Henry Arthur Jones

Carnac Sahib

An Original Play in Four Acts

Henry Arthur Jones

Carnac Sahib
An Original Play in Four Acts

ISBN/EAN: 9783337063245

Printed in Europe, USA, Canada, Australia, Japan

Cover: Foto ©Andreas Hilbeck / pixelio.de

More available books at **www.hansebooks.com**

CARNAC SAHIB

AN ORIGINAL PLAY
IN FOUR ACTS

BY

HENRY ARTHUR JONES

AUTHOR OF

'THE TEMPTER,' 'MICHAEL AND HIS LOST ANGEL,' 'THE LIARS,'
'THE CRUSADERS,' 'THE MASQUERADERS,' 'JUDAH,' 'THE
CASE OF REBELLIOUS SUSAN,' 'THE DANCING GIRL,'
'THE MIDDLEMAN,' 'THE ROGUE'S COMEDY,'
'THE PHYSICIAN,' 'THE TRIUMPH OF
THE PHILISTINES,' 'THE
MANŒUVRES OF JANE,'
'THE GOAL,'
ETC.

New York

THE MACMILLAN COMPANY

LONDON: MACMILLAN & CO., LTD.

1899

PERSONS REPRESENTED

COLONEL STACEY CARNAC.
COLONEL ARTHUR SYRETT.
GENERAL SIR HARDINGE SCRIVENER.
MAJOR HEDLEY KYNASTON.
MAJOR WILLIAM RADNAGE.
REVEREND JIMMY HOBBS.
MR. FORD.
THE MAHARAJAH OF MOTIALA.
CAPTAIN BELL.
LIEUTENANT RICHARD BARTON.
LIEUTENANT ALAN LOVATT.
MAHOMET ALI.
MIRZA KHAN.
ALI KHAN.
CHRISTNA.
BETTS.

ELLICE FORD.
MAY FORD.
AMINA.
MRS. CARMICHAEL.
MRS. REMINGTON.
MRS. WHITMORE.
MADGE LOVELACE.
SEETA.
OLIVE ARNISON.

*Indian Soldiers, Native Soldiers, Shop-
keepers, Populace.*

(v)

ACT I.

SCENE — 1. Compound of Colonel Carnac's Bungalow and Office at Dilghaut. (Morning.)

2. Ruined Hindoo Temple near Fyzapore. (The same night.)

3. Exterior of Olive Arnison's Bungalow at Dilghaut. (Sunrise the next morning.)

(A fortnight passes.)

ACT II.

SCENE — Grounds of the English Club at Dilghaut. (Night.)

(Ten days pass.)

ACT III.

SCENE — 1. Room in Colonel Carnac's Bungalow at Dilghaut. (Morning.)

2. Bazaar and Exterior of the Ghur-i-Noor, Dilghaut. (The same afternoon.)

3. Room in Colonel Carnac's Bungalow. (Night.)

(Nearly three weeks pass.)

ACT IV.

SCENE — 1. The Jewelled Palace at Fyzapore. (Sunset.)

2. Room in Olive Arnison's Bungalow at Dilghaut. (Evening.)

3. The Jewelled Palace. (Night. The falling of the curtain signifies the passing of the night.)

4. The Jewelled Palace. (Dawn.)

The scene is laid at the cities of Fyzapore and Dilghaut, in India, at the present time.

ACT I

SCENE I

THE VERANDA AND COMPOUND OF COLONEL STACEY CARNAC'S BUNGALOW AT DILGHAUT

Discover LIEUTENANT DICKY BARTON, LIEUTENANT ALAN LOVATT, *and* MAJOR RADNAGE, *Indian Medical Staff, and, at some little distance,* MAJOR HEDLEY KYNASTON.

LOVATT. You may say what you like against her, but Olive Arnison is a devilish fascinating woman.

BARTON. I hadn't been five minutes in her company before I felt I should do any fool's trick she asked me, and say "Thank you."

LOVATT. It's a wonderful power that some women have — the Lady Hamilton power of making a silly fool of every man they come across. And Olive Arnison has got it.

RADNAGE (*a good-humoured, witty, rhetorical, clever, broken-down man of fifty-five* — "*Nobody's enemy but his own*"). So has every good-looking woman.

B

BARTON. Oh no, Billy. There are some beautiful women that freeze you like an iceberg. And there are others, by Jove, if they'd only be kind enough to walk over you and wipe their pretty little shoes on you, you'd love them all the more for it, bless their hearts.

RADNAGE (*pompous, florid, mock-oratorical. He has had several glasses*). My son Richard, the philosophy of this matter lies in a nut-shell. Given any one of these divine creatures with beauty, the question arises, "Hath she also virtue?" For then her beauty is naught; it is dead and cold; it hath no pulse or relish of life in it. But, given any one of these divine creatures with beauty, and let that beauty be easy of access, marketable, benign, and of sovereign comfort to the wayfaring rapscallion, man (*pointing to himself*), then is he fired to his destiny. He hastens to be her slave, and goeth rejoicingly to red ruin and blue damnation for her sake. Virtue, my son Richard, is a deadly and nauseous enemy to beauty. And for all our treble rhinoceros-hide of damnable hypocrisy, we Englishmen know it. And act upon it! Tell me, my son Richard, who lies snuggest and warmest in the hearts of the English people, Nell Gwynne or Hannah More? Find me one tolerably attractive virtuous woman in all the roll-call

of history, and I will own to you that in par-
celling out the capacious freehold of my heart
in small residential plots for these divine creatures to build upon and inhabit, I have made
a mistake, and I stand before you at fifty-five,
socially, morally, spiritually, and professionally,
a failure, a ghastly and lamentable failure, a
wreck and a ruin !   (*Drinks.*)

KYNASTON (*has been away from the group, but
early in the previous conversation has turned to
listen to it, unnoticed by them. He now comes
forward to them, a handsome, manly Englishman,
rather under forty, with a very open, winning,
candid face. Speaks very quietly*).   And aren't
you a failure, a wreck, and a ruin, Billy?

RADNAGE (*ashamed*).   Kynaston !

KYNASTON.   And isn't it enough for you to
have made a mess of your own life, old boy,
but you must needs show these youngsters the
way to make a mess of theirs?   Don't believe
him, you lads !   It's a lie that there's any
lasting happiness apart from a pure and virtuous woman !   Take my word for it.   No,
take his, for he has made the experiment.
Billy, tell them again what you are at fifty-
five.

RADNAGE (*much ashamed*).   I'm sorry, Kynaston !   He's right, my boys !   Take godly advice
from him and an awful warning from me.   It's

all I'm fit for! Upon my soul, Kynaston, I'm awfully sorry!

> (*Shambles off ashamed, half whistling a few notes to hide his discomfiture. Exit.*)

KYNASTON. You were dining at Lady Scrivener's last night, Dicky. Did you see anything of the quarrel between Carnac and Syrett?

BARTON. Yes. All through the dinner Mrs. Arnison was cooing and flirting with Syrett. Carnac watched them for a few minutes, looking as grim as old Nick. Then he began to talk; chaffed Syrett unmercifully; got Mrs. Arnison's attention, and kept the ball rolling till the ladies left the room.

KYNASTON. And then?

BARTON. We had a bad quarter of an hour till we got into the drawing-room. Then Carnac went straight up to Mrs. Arnison, got her to sing, and Syrett never spoke a word all the rest of the evening till he got outside.

KYNASTON. What then?

LOVATT. They began sparring. It was all we could do to keep them apart.

BARTON. I dragged Carnac off to the club and sat drinking whisky with him till three this morning.

LOVATT. I went back with Syrett to his bungalow.

BARTON. Awkward, an affair of this kind

coming just now when the General's away, and all this bother with the natives.

Enter the REVEREND JIMMY HOBBS, *a round-faced, good-tempered, jolly-looking young English clergyman, with nothing clerical about him except his dress.*

HOBBS.   I say, you fellows, this is getting serious.

BARTON.   What's getting serious, Padri ?

HOBBS.   Well, you know, though I am a clergyman, I never interfere in my neighbours' business.   But somebody ought to say a word to Carnac and Syrett, or—only it would be such a sneakish thing to do—give a hint to Arnison to come here and look after his wife.

LOVATT.   Oh, Arnison knows all about it.

BARTON.   It's six of one and half-a-dozen of the other.   Arnison has always done as he pleases, so now he's obliged to let her do as she pleases.

HOBBS.   It's a thousand pities for Carnac.

BARTON.   Let's hope we shall get a jolly good set-to in a day or two with the natives, and that will take Carnac's mind off her.

LOVATT (*to* KYNASTON).   What do you think, Major?   We shall have a brush with them soon, sha'n't we ?

KYNASTON. Carnac's going to move this afternoon, I believe, if the news is favourable for a night attack.

BARTON. Good! By Jove, I long to get at the devils.

Enter ALI KHAN, CARNAC'S *orderly, from bungalow. He salutes.*

ALI. Carnac Sahib sends his salaam. Will all Officers Sahibs please go to Carnac Sahib in his office?

KYNASTON. Is there any fresh news?

ALI. Carnac Sahib has just received very important telegraphic message.

(ALI *salaams and exit into bungalow.*)

BARTON (*digging* HOBBS *in the ribs*). I say Padri, you rank old duffer, aren't you sorry you're going to be out of this?

HOBBS. I'm not sure I shall be out of it, Dicky. But I shall do my duty, whether it happens to be an odd job of fighting, or reading the burial service over you!

(*Exeunt* BARTON *and* LOVATT *into bunga-low.* KYNASTON *is following, when enter into the compound* COLONEL SY-RETT. SYRETT *is a thin, severe, sharp-featured man about forty, taciturn and outwardly cold.*)

KYNASTON.   The Colonel has just had an important telegram. He has sent for us to go to him.

SYRETT.   Has he?

KYNASTON.   Won't you come in?

SYRETT.   Yes, when I'm ready.

                    (*Enter* KYNASTON *into bungalow.*)

HOBBS.   I say, Syrett—you won't misunderstand me?

SYRETT.   Go on.

HOBBS.   Two jolly good fellows, old friends of mine and old friends of each other, are getting at loggerheads about a—well, if I wasn't a parson I should say she was a—well, I should call her a—well, everything that isn't polite. But I'll simply say she's a lady who is bound to bring one or the other or both of these jolly good fellows to trouble and disgrace if they don't cut her.

SYRETT.   Let us hope that *one* of these jolly good fellows will cut the lady, or that she will cut him.

HOBBS.   And the other?

SYRETT.   The other doesn't need your advice, Padri.

Enter into the compound OLIVE ARNISON, *a supple, soft-voiced, fascinating woman about thirty.*

OLIVE.   Good morning, Colonel Syrett. Good Morning, Mr. Hobbs.

HOBBS (*curtly*).   Good morning.

OLIVE.   Am I in your way?

HOBBS.   Not in mine, I assure you.

(*Exit.*)

OLIVE.   There is some fresh news, isn't there?

SYRETT.   Yes, I believe Carnac's had an important telegram.   You aren't alarmed?

OLIVE.   No.   There's no danger for us poor fluttering she-things?

SYRETT.   Do you think I'd let you stay here a moment if there were.

OLIVE (*eagerly*).   But there will be some fighting?

SYRETT.   Yes.   A good sharp tussle.   It's only a matter of smashing the Rajah and hanging a few hundred natives.

OLIVE.   And that will be easy work for Colonel Carnac?

SYRETT.   You think so.

OLIVE.   Yes.   His record is such a splendid one.   And I hear that he has the same power over men that he has over women.

SYRETT.   Has he power over women?

OLIVE.   I've heard so.   You ought to know. You're one of his oldest friends, aren't you?

SYRETT.   We were friends.

OLIVE,   Aren't you friends now?

SYRETT.   I'd kill my brother like a dog if he

stood between me and you. (OLIVE *laughs.*) Why do you laugh ?

OLIVE. I love to hear men talk. The first time I came out a silly boy swore to jump overboard if I didn't promise to marry him in three weeks. The next morning I asked him why he was at breakfast. He showed me a razor that he had sharpened, and swore he would do it that way, outside my cabin door.

SYRETT. Well ? What happened?

OLIVE. He was exquisitely shaved for the rest of the voyage, and behaved very badly to a governess the moment we landed at Calcutta.

SYRETT. You wish to see me sharpen my razor?

OLIVE. For whose throat ?

SYRETT. Mine — or yours — or his ?

OLIVE. Oh don't be so impartially bloodthirsty. Go and kill a few dozen natives, and let that satisfy you.

SYRETT. You don't think I should keep my vow ?

OLIVE (*looks at him very intently for a few seconds*). Yes. I think you would. So pray don't make one.

SYRETT. But if I have already made one ?

OLIVE. Then I've been more foolish and

thoughtless than I intended. But it's only for a few days more.

SYRETT. Only for a few days more ?

OLIVE. My husband writes me that his survey will be finished in another week, and he expects me to join him at Simla as soon as possible. Meantime, he is sending his sister to take care of me.

SYRETT. But you won't go ?

OLIVE (*smiles*). Not till I've seen Colonel Carnac smash the Rajah.

SYRETT. If I were in command instead of him ——

OLIVE. Ah ! You envy him !

SYRETT. No. Promise me that if there's a good fight you won't shilly-shally with me any longer, and I'll promise you that I'll either get killed, or I'll come back and make you proud of what I've done for you.

OLIVE (*intensely pleased*). Can I make you fight ?

SYRETT. You sha'n't ask me that if I come back alive. And if I do, there's only one thing· I'll ask of you, and I'll only take one answer.

Enter MAHOMET ALI, *bearer to* SYRETT.
MAHOMET *salaams very respectfully*.

MAHOMET. Carnac Sahib sent his pig of a

servant to command you to his presence. I
said you were not at home, and sent the pig
back to his master. The pig come back to
me and say he must see you.

SYRETT. What did you say?

MAHOMET. I say I know not where to
find you, and I drive the pig away from the
door.

Enter from the bungalow STACEY CARNAC, *a man
rather over forty. He is a handsome man in
the prime of life, his face giving signs that he
has " lived." He and* SYRETT *stand looking at
each other.* MAHOMET *salaams to* CARNAC, *then
turns very submissively to* SYRETT.

MAHOMET (*to* SYRETT). Carnac Sahib command the Sahib Syrett to attend him at once.
What answer shall I make to Carnac Sahib?

SYRETT (*to* MAHOMET). Say that I'll come
at the earliest moment convenient.

MAHOMET (*goes with great respect to* CARNAC).
Syrett Sahib will attend Carnac Sahib at the
earliest moment convenient.

CARNAC (*taking* MAHOMET *by the throat.
Shaking him*). Listen! This is the second
time you've dared to insult my servant. The
next time a good stout English rope will go —
queek — round this Oriental neck of yours.

(*Shaking him by the throat.*) Queek! (*Kicks him.*)

> (MAHOMET, *having recovered his balance, is going off, turns and looks with deadly hatred at* CARNAC *for a moment, then salaams profoundly to* CARNAC *and* SYRETT, *and exit.*)

SYRETT. Carnac, that man is my servant——

CARNAC. Then, my dear fellow, teach him to behave himself.

SYRETT. I am responsible for his behaviour.

CARNAC. Then it will be the more easily corrected. (*Turns to* OLIVE.) Mrs. Arnison, I'm afraid this rising will be a stiffer bit of business than we bargained for. I've just been talking with Lady Scrivener, and I've decided to send all you ladies to Barat.

OLIVE. But what can we do there?

CARNAC. Wait until the General comes with reinforcements.

OLIVE. But Colonel Syrett says there's no danger here.

CARNAC. Colonel Syrett is scarcely in a position to judge.

SYRETT. Are you keeping important information to yourself, sir?

CARNAC. Till General Scrivener comes up I'm in command here, and I act upon my own responsibility.

SYRETT. It's scarcely regular, is it, sir, to consult the ladies of the Station rather than your next in command?

CARNAC. I consult neither the ladies nor my next in command. In a matter of their safety I expect them to obey me, and (*turning to* OLIVE) I'm sure they will. In a matter of discipline (*turning to* SYRETT) I expect him to obey me, and I'll take good care that he does.

SYRETT (*with a shrug of the shoulders, to* OLIVE). I'm afraid Mrs. Arnison, that when my superior officer cannot enforce a particular kind of obedience from a lady, he revenges himself by trying to exact an absurd amount from his subordinates.

CARNAC (*fires up, then with perfect self-control throws a stern glance of warning at* SYRETT). My dear Arthur, I never have occasion to enforce obedience from ladies — I always find that their wishes perfectly coincide with my own, and (*glancing at* OLIVE) I don't think my luck is going to desert me now. Mrs. Arnison, let me take you over to Lady Scrivener.

OLIVE. No. How is it that I always make you two quarrel?

CARNAC. There's no quarrel on my side. (*To* OLIVE.) Time presses——

OLIVE. No, I'd rather stay. I've been out eight years and I've never seen any fighting.

CARNAC. You'll scarcely see any fighting if you do stay. But you'll most likely see some very ugly sights.

OLIVE. Ugly sights?

CARNAC. Wounded men — dead men — natives being hanged ——

OLIVE. How horrid! Still I'd rather stay ——

CARNAC. Believe me, it's dangerous.

OLIVE (*turns to* SYRETT). Colonel Syrett, do you think it's dangerous?

CARNAC. I beg Colonel Syrett won't use any further words.

SYRETT. I won't sir. But you may find me in your way when it comes to deeds.

CARNAC (*with great warning*). I hope not, Arthur, for your sake. Now, Mrs. Arnison ——

OLIVE. No, you shan't go. Colonel Syrett, you come with me to Lady Scrivener.

SYRETT (*delighted*). By all means.

(*Going off with her.*)

CARNAC. Syrett ——

SYRETT. Well, sir?

CARNAC. Please tell Lady Scrivener that I send all the ladies of the Station to Barat this afternoon, and ask her to be good enough to be ready at two.

OLIVE. Indeed (*turns to* SYRETT). I won't trouble you to come with me, Colonel Syrett.

Stay and help Colonel Carnac plan this night attack. I'm sure there's no danger here.

CARNAC. Believe me, there is — a little.

OLIVE. A little danger? But that's delightful. I want to have ten minutes — no, half-an-hour's delicious fright. I want to feel that our lives are in your hands, and if you make the least little slip we may all be massacred. Oh, I want to feel it! And then to escape by a miracle, and to welcome you both, back just as it grows light to-morrow morning, with, perhaps, a little wound apiece, eh? Don't you think George Edgecombe looks all the handsomer for that slash across his forehead? Well, just a handsome little wound like that. Not dangerous, at least not very dangerous. (*Going off*, *turns*.) Will one of you get wounded, do you think? Isn't it horrid of me to talk like this? Of course, you won't get wounded, will you? (*Exit*.)

CARNAC. Why did you tell Mrs. Arnison she's in no danger here?

SYRETT. Believe me, sir, Mrs. Arnison is in no danger while she's near to me.

CARNAC. Syrett, take care. You are presuming on our old friendship. Yesterday you went far enough to justify me in placing you under arrest.

SYRETT. But you won't, Stacey.

CARNAC. Do you challenge me ?

SYRETT. Yes, you daren't.

CARNAC. I daren't.

SYRETT. You daren't let it be said through-out the service, and throughout India, that you were mean enough to put me under arrest be-cause you were afraid I should be your suc-cessful rival with a woman.

Enter KYNASTON.

CARNAC. You're right. People might say that. (*Very contemptuously.*) You might say it, too. I won't give you the chance.

KYNASTON. What's the matter ?

SYRETT. He talks about putting me under arrest — to get me out of his way with a lady. What do you say to that ?

KYNASTON. I say that both of you are senseless and cowardly to wrangle about a woman at such a moment as this, when every thought and every energy are wanted for this business. And such a woman ! Why she's no better than ——

CARNAC. Stop that, Hedley !

KYNASTON. But you've heard of that affair last year ——

CARNAC. Stop, I say. Not another word about her.

KYNASTON. But are you mad, both of you ? To fly at each other's throats when everything depends upon our keeping together and working for our very lives. The rising is spreading ; we don't know where it may break out next. Stacey, think. If there are such things as duty and honour ——

CARNAC (*lighting a cigarette*). Cut that twaddle, my dear old psalm-singer. I'm going to do my duty, and I'll take care of my honour. (*Turns to* SYRETT.) Look here, Arthur, we'll sink our private differences and carry through this business like gentlemen. And when this scrimmage is over we'll see who's best man with her. Meantime we fight fair.

SYRETT. Very well.

CARNAC. Shake hands on it. (SYRETT *gives his hand very reluctantly. They shake hands.*) Go up to the lines and see that everything is ready for to-night.

SYRETT. Yes, sir. (*Going off.*)

CARNAC (*calls to him*). We fight fair, Arthur?

SYRETT (*as he goes off*). We fight fair, Stacey. (*Exit.*)

KYNASTON. You fight fair for a woman who isn't worth a thought or a wish from either of you. There's better fighting than that to do just now, Stacey.

c

CARNAC. Yes, and I sha'n't do it any the worse for having a woman at the back of me. And whether she's good or bad doesn't matter a curse. Don't look shocked, old fellow. It's the nature of this beast.

KYNASTON. You wouldn't have spoken like that when Enid was alive.

CARNAC (*very softly*). And we should have been really brothers if she had lived.

KYNASTON. The last few months I've been glad, Stacey, that she didn't.

CARNAC (*moved*). You're right. I daresay I should have broken her heart. But I did love her, Hedley.

KYNASTON. Then for her sake give up this woman.

CARNAC. No.

KYNASTON. You won't?

CARNAC. No. Oh, my dear old boy, what's the use of fussing about a woman? Or a dozen? Or a thousand, for that matter? I can always collar myself and keep them at a safe distance.

KYNASTON. What do you call a safe distance?

CARNAC. When fighting's the business, ten thousand miles. When love's the business, not the ten-thousandth part of an inch.

Enter OLIVE.

KYNASTON (*glancing at* OLIVE). I'm sorry,
Stacey.   (*Going off.*)

CORNAC (*calling him*). Hedley ! This won't
change our friendship, old fellow ?

KYNASTON (*offering hand*). Nothing can
change our friendship, Stacey.

(*A warm handshake.* OLIVE *comes up,
bows to* KYNASTON, *who bows coldly to
her, and exits.*)

OLIVE (*triumphantly*). I've been to Lady
Scrivener. I've persuaded her to stay.

CARNAC. Then I must persuade you both
to go.

OLIVE. How ?

CARNAC. By the gentlest means that can be
employed to get you there.

OLIVE. I want so much to stay and see the
fighting. I may stay ? (*He shakes his head.*)
Yes ?

CARNAC. No.

OLIVE (*with great insinuation*). If Colonel
Syrett were in command — he would let me
stay. He knows that women can be brave.

CARNAC. And I know that they can be —
women.

OLIVE. Don't you want me to see you come
in triumphant to-morrow morning, just as it
grows light ?

CARNAC. I want to be sure that you are safe. Then I shall be sure of myself in the scrimmage to-night.

OLIVE (*in the same tone and words that she had used to* COLONEL SYRETT *in the earlier scene*). Can I make you fight ?

CARNAC. You know that you can make me do anything.

OLIVE. Can I ?

CARNAC. Anything that does not touch my honour.

OLIVE (*impatiently*). Oh, honour, honour, honour ! What a silly, tiresome word ! You pretend to love me !

CARNAC. Pretend ?

OLIVE. Then let me stay.

CARNAC. No.

OLIVE (*flashes round on him*). I won't go. Do you hear ? I will stay here.

CARNAC (*takes her two wrists and shakes her with grim playfulness, half tender, half stern. Very firmly*). Listen. I love you. And when this is over I'll make you love me. But, meantime, you'll go to Barat this afternoon. You'll go, my charming rebel, if I have to strap these pretty limbs of yours to the gharry and drive you there myself, to the music of your screams all the fifteen miles. Now do you understand that I mean you shall go ?

OLIVE. Yes! And I love you, Stacey Carnac, for making me go. You're a braver man than Colonel Syrett, after all.

Enter HOBBS *with* BETTS, *an English soldier.*

CARNAC. Well, Padri?

HOBBS. I beg pardon, sir, but here's one of the Fyzapore men.

CARNAC (*to* SOLDIER). What is it?

BETTS. Despatch from Mr. Ford, sir.

Enter KYNASTON. CARNAC *takes despatch, opens it eagerly, shows surprise and angry impatience.*

KYNASTON. Anything the matter sir?

CARNAC. The Nawab of Fyzapore has broken out. All the Englishmen have had to fly for their lives. Ford and his daughter have escaped into the country. It couldn't have happened at a worse time. (*Takes out watch.*) Half-past twelve. There's no time to be lost. They must be rescued at once. (*To* SOLDIER.) Do you know where Mr. Ford and the English ladies are now?

BETTS. They were making off towards Lalserai, sir. We shall find them hiding somewhere about there.

CARNAC. How long will it take to get there?

BETTS. It has taken me three hours to come over, sir.

HOBBS. If you're going over, sir, perhaps you wouldn't mind my riding with you. You're short of men, and I may come in handy for something or the other.

CARNAC. Very well, Padri. But first tell Mr. Barton I want him here at once.

HOBBS. Right, sir.   (*Exit.*)

CARNAC (*to* SOLDIER). Go and get something to eat, and be ready to take us to Mr. Ford in a quarter of an hour.

BETTS. Yes, sir.   (*Exit.*)

CARNAC. Kynaston, tell your company to fall in at once.

KYNASTON. Yes, sir.

> (*Exit.* CARNAC *walks up and down in indecision.*)

OLIVE. What's the matter?

CARNAC. Ford must be relieved at once. I don't know whether to send Syrett in command or to go myself.

OLIVE. Why let Colonel Syrett have the honour of rescuing these beautiful maidens in distress?

CARNAC. Beautiful maidens!

OLIVE. Miss Ford is young and beautiful, isn't she?

CARNAC. Is she? It doesn't matter what she is. If I go, I leave Colonel Syrett here in command.

OLIVE. Well?

CARNAC. And you're here.

OLIVE. But I'm to leave for Barat this afternoon.

CARNAC. You'll be here some time with him before you start. Promise me if I go—oh! I'm a mad, jealous fool—Promise me you won't speak to Syrett while I'm away.

OLIVE. Not speak to him?

CARNAC. I'm going to Fyzapore for your sake.

OLIVE. Is it for me? Is it?

CARNAC. Yes. And I can't bear to leave you a moment with Syrett. You won't speak to him while I'm gone? (*She laughs.*) Ah! I won't be so small. (*Snaps his finger.*) Do as you please. Let him win you if he can. (*Going off.*) Good-bye!

OLIVE. Colonel Carnac! (*He stops.*) Since you wish it, I won't speak to Colonel Syrett while you're away.

CARNAC. You swear?

OLIVE (*giving him her hand*). I swear.

CARNAC. Thanks. (*Kisses her hand.*) I shall do something now!

Enter SYRETT.

SYRETT (*to* OLIVE).   Are you going to run away to Barat ?   Or are you going to be brave and stay ?   (OLIVE *does not reply.*)   Won't you speak to me ?

> (OLIVE *puts her finger on her lip.* SY-
> RETT *looks to* CARNAC *for an expla-
> nation.*)

Enter BARTON.

CARNAC (*to* SYRETT, *glancing at* OLIVE, *grate-
ful and delighted*).   Arthur, the Nawab of Fyza-
pore has broken out and hunted all Europeans from the town.   I am taking Kynaston and his company to rescue Ford and the ladies.   I shall be back to lead the attack against the Rajah. (SYRETT *is looking at* OLIVE, *surprised at her silence.*)   Do you hear me ?

SYRETT.   Yes, sir.

CARNAC.   Mr. Barton, you'll take all the ladies of the Station with an escort to Barat. Be sure you see them in safety there.

BARTON.   Yes, sir.

CARNAC.   Start at once, and be back at ten to-night to join the night attack.

BARTON.   Yes, sir.

Enter KYNASTON.

CARNAC.   All ready, Kynaston ?

KYNASTON. Yes, sir.

CARNAC. I'm going to lead myself. (*To* OLIVE.) Good-bye.

OLIVE. Good-bye.

CARNAC. Colonel Syrett, have everything ready for me at ten to-night.

SYRETT. Yes, sir.

CARNAC. Now, Kynaston ——

(*Exit, followed by* KYNASTON.)

BARTON (*to* OLIVE). You ladies ought to be packing.

OLIVE. We needn't start till two.

BARTON. The Colonel said we were to start at once.

OLIVE. Oh, is there any hurry?

BARTON. Yes, I think. You see, if we don't get off at once I sha'n't be back in time for the attack to-night, and I don't want to be out of it. (*To* SYRETT.) Don't you think the ladies ought to start at once, sir?

SYRETT. I don't think they need start at all. Do you, Mrs. Arnison?

(OLIVE *does not reply, but smiles and puts her finger on her lip.*)

Enter CAPTAIN BELL, *in great haste and excitement.*

BELL. Is the Colonel here, sir?

SYRETT. I'm in command here. What's the matter?

BELL. I've been reconnoitring round Blakepore, sir. The Rajah is creeping up to us. I feel sure he means to attack us this afternoon.

SYRETT (*suddenly elated with an idea*). The Rajah means to attack us this afternoon? Good! Good!

BARTON (*starting off*). Shall I go and tell Colonel Carnac?

SYRETT. No. Stay.

BARTON. But he hasn't left the lines. Hadn't I better let him know.

SYRETT. What for? I'm in command here. (*To* BELL.) The Rajah's just the other side of Blakepore, you say?

BELL. Yes, sir. We ought to be formed at once to be ready for him.

SYRETT. Very well.

BARTON. Mrs. Arnison, I'll get you ladies away at once.

SYRETT. No, Barton. I shall want every man here. I'm going to attack the Rajah this afternoon before he attacks us.

BARTON. Without letting Colonel Carnac know, sir?

SYRETT. I'll let Colonel Carnac know—in good time.

SYRETT (*to* OLIVE).   There will be some fighting at Blakepore, perhaps nearer.   Are you afraid to stay?   (*She shakes her head.*) You'd rather stay?   (*She nods.*)

SYRETT (*to* BARTON).   Go and tell Lady Scrivener that the ladies will not go to Barat.

BARTON.   Yes, sir.   (*Exit.*)

SYRETT (*to* BELL).   Go to the lines and tell Major Hartford to parade all the men at once.

BELL.   Yes, sir.   (*Exit.*)

SYRETT (*to* OLIVE).   You wish to stay? (*She nods.*)   It's dangerous.   (*She smiles.*)   Why won't you speak?   (*She smiles and shakes her head.   Savagely.*)   Carnac has closed your lips? (*She smiles and nods.*)   When he returns he'll find I've smashed the Rajah for him, and saved him the trouble.   Shall I win?

(OLIVE *nods very emphatically.*)

SYRETT.   Wish me luck.   (OLIVE *nods and smiles.*)   Give me that rose.

> (*He is about to take the rose, but she shakes her head, puts her hand to restrain him from taking the rose, and offers him her lips with sudden abandonment; he kisses her; she then imperiously points to him to go.   Exit* SYRETT.   *She stands waving him an adieu.   Scene closed in by Scene 2.*)

Scene II

A Ruined Indian Temple. Front Scene to Set
in Front of Scene I

*At back, crumbling wall of old marble covered with
weather-stains, moss, and vegetation. Crumbling
wall to the R., with a little broken entrance. To
the L., a wall with an archway as if at the top
of steps. A large seat in the masonry, L. A
large branch of a tree comes through a hole at
the bottom of the wall, R. The time is night.
Occasional shouts and cries in the distance.
Stray shots. Bugle calls. Flickers of light come
occasionally through the opening, R., as if from
houses burning in the distance.*

Discover Ellice Ford *and* Amina, *her Ayah.* Ellice
*is ordinarily a very bright, attractive, laughing
English girl of twenty; she is now dishevelled, her
dress is torn, her hair disordered, and she shows
signs of fatigue and anxiety. The Ayah is a
Mahommedan woman about twenty-five. Flickers
of the conflagration come fitfully through the opening in wall and light up their faces.*

Ellice (*steals to opening,* R.). They're burning another house, Major Weston's!

Amina. Come away, Miss Sahib; they'll
see your face.

ELLICE. There's another beginning to smoke. It's our own! Isn't it? Look!

AMINA (*peeping out*). Yes, dear Miss Sahib! Come away!

ELLICE. Oh the fiends! And my little May! If they should touch her — oh, Ayah, tell me that my darling is safe, even if you don't believe it.

AMINA. Don't fret, Miss Sahib. Your noble father is sure to find the dear little Miss Sahib and bring her to you.

ELLICE (*in a frightened whisper*). But my father may be killed himself! And the other ladies, Madge Lovelace and the rest — how did they manage to get parted from us?

AMINA. Oh, Miss Sahib, it's a mercy that any of us are alive.

(*Sounds of distant shots occasionally.*)

ELLICE. Do you think we might risk it and venture out?

AMINA. No, no, Miss Sahib. Your noble father command us stay here till he come to rescue us.

ELLICE. But if Colonel Carnac hasn't rescued him! That must have been Colonel Carnac and his men who came up and drove the Nawab's men back?

AMINA. Yes, surely that was the noble Carnac Sahib.

ELLICE. Then why doesn't he come? They surely won't leave us all night in this place. (*Peeping out of opening.*) Look! Aren't those soldiers creeping behind those trees? Ah! they're going away!

(*Tramp of retreating men at a distance, and then silence.*)

AMINA. Come and rest a little while, Miss Sahib, and when your noble father comes you will be ready to march again.

ELLICE (*reclining on seat*). March? Oh, why doesn't Colonel Carnac come?

AMINA. He is very brave, this Carnac Sahib?

ELLICE. Oh, yes. I met him at Simuri the year before last, just after he had done that splendid forced march to Kurghan. I danced with him twice at my first ball out here. And a week after I met him near the rope bridge over the river. They said the bridge wasn't safe, and I daren't cross it. When Colonel Carnac saw I was afraid, he came up and offered to help me over. So I thanked him, and he put his arm round me and told me to shut my eyes and not to open them till I was safe on the other side. But I didn't feel a bit afraid. I knew I was safe with him. So when we were half way over I opened my eyes and there we were, swing-

ing, swinging, swinging, with the river roaring
five hundred feet below us, and only those bits
of rope to save us from being dashed to
pieces.   Oh, it was delightful — and now!
Oh, why doesn't he come? (*Shouts and a
bugle call.   Tramp of approaching men.*)   Hark!
What's that?

AMINA (*looking off* L., *listening*).   Some men
coming.

ELLICE (*breathless*).   Are   they   English?
Are   they   English?

AMINA.   Hush, Miss Sahib.

> (*The two women listen in an agony of
> terror, and cling together and with-
> draw into the opening,* R. *Noise of
> feet tramping up the staircase.*)

Enter, L., CARNAC, HOBBS, LOVATT, OFFICERS,
        BETTS, *and* SOLDIERS.

CARNAC.   Bring me that light.   (SOLDIER
brings him a lantern.)   Is anyone here?

ELLICE (*coming out of opening*).   Colonel Carnac, is it you?

CARNAC.   Yes.   Who is it?

> (*Holding light to her face.*)

ELLICE.   Don't you know me?

CARNAC.   No, who are you?

ELLICE.   Ellice Ford.

CARNAC (*carelessly*). That's all right. We were looking for you.

ELLICE (*very disappointed*). You don't remember me ?

CARNAC. No. (*Holding lantern in her face.*) Oh, yes, I helped you across the rope bridge. I'd forgotten.

ELLICE. We met several times the year before last.

CARNAC. Did we ? I don't remember.

ELLICE. I've been expecting you all the afternoon.

CARNAC. I ought to have been here three hours ago, but the Nawab gave me a lot of trouble. Now I'm going to send you back to Dilghaut. Can you start at once ?

ELLICE. My father ? Is he safe ?

CARNAC. Yes, he'll be here in a moment.

ELLICE. And my little sister and the other ladies ?

CARNAC. Haven't seen anything of them. Now, are you ready to start ?

ELLICE (*bursting into tears of relief*). Oh, I thought they would leave us to die here. I thought you'd never come !

CARNAC (*takes out watch*). Past seven o'clock. Come, come, you mustn't cry.

ELLICE. I won't. I shall be better directly. (*She sobs a little in* AMINA'S *arms.*)

CARNAC. I can give you just thirty seconds to recover, and another thirty seconds to prepare for your journey.

ELLICE. I'm ready. Can I say good-bye to my father ?

CARNAC. Not unless he comes at once. Oh ! here he is.

Enter MR. FORD, *the Commissioner at Fyzapore, an Englishman between fifty and sixty, armed.*

CARNAC. Oh, Ford, here you are. Where's Kynaston ?

FORD. Hasn't he got here, sir ?

CARNAC. No, I thought he was with your party.

FORD. No, sir. We got parted just as we were peppering those beggars in the palms.

CARNAC (*still looking at watch*). I must be back to Dilghaut at ten to lead the night attack. Now listen. You must hold Fyzapore at any cost.

FORD. Yes, sir.

CARNAC. I'll leave you Kynaston and his company. When he turns up, take him back with you. The palace is the best place to defend. Tell him to hold it until I can relieve you.

FORD. Yes, sir.

D

CARNAC. Where are the other ladies?

FORD. I can't say, sir. My youngest girl is with them. We shall find them in safety somewhere, I hope.

CARNAC. Send them to Dilghaut if you can do so without risk. If that's impossible, take them back to Fyzapore. I'll send Miss Ford on to Dilghaut. (*To* ELLICE.) You'll be safe there with Lady Scrivener.

ELLICE. But my father and little sister? Oughtn't I to stay with you?

FORD. No, no, my dear, you'll be safer at Dilghaut.

> (ELLICE *and her father stand aside and are seen to be saying good-bye to each other.*)

CARNAC. Mr. Lovatt, go and see if the palkis are ready for Miss Ford and her Ayah. You will please escort her to Dilghaut.

LOVATT. Yes, sir.   (*Exit.*)

ELLICE (*to* FORD). Give my dearest, dearest love to May. Tell her if she can't come to me at Dilghaut, I'll come to her at Fyzapore as soon as they'll let me.

> (CARNAC *has been looking at his watch, chafing with impatience.*)

CARNAC. Miss Ford, if you start at once I can put you safely on the high road. (*A noise outside.*) What's that? Kynaston! (*Looking*

off L.   KYNASTON *staggers in, wounded.*)   My
dear fellow!   It's not serious?   Say it's not
serious, Hedley!

KYNASTON.   I don't know.   Don't bother
about me.

CARNAC.   But I must.   I'll take you back
with me?

KYNASTON.   I couldn't hold out.   You go
and smash the Rajah, and leave me to pull
through if I can.

CARNAC (*to* HOBBS).   Padri!   take the great-
est care of Major Kynaston.   I'll send Radnage out to him the moment I get back.
Ford, you will see that everything is done for
Major Kynaston?

FORD.   Yes, sir.

CARNAC (*to* KYNASTON).   Good-bye, old fellow——

KYNASTON.   Good-bye —— Don't wait.

Enter LOVATT.

LOVATT.   The palkis are waiting for Miss
Ford.

CARNAC.   Now Miss Ford, now Ayah.
        (*Exit* CARNAC — *exit* AYAH, L.)

ELLICE.   Good-bye, father.   I can't bear to
leave you.   Oh, if we should never meet
again!

FORD.   We shall meet again, dear, either on
this earth or ——

LOVATT.   If you're ready, Miss Ford.

ELLICE.   Quite ready.

> (*Throws her father a last agonized look,
> and exit,* L., *followed by* LOVATT.   *A
> moment's pause.*   FORD *returns to*
> KYNASTON.)

CARNAC (*re-entering hurriedly, goes up to*
KYNASTON).   Hedley, my dear old fellow—I
can't leave you.   I'll carry you with me on my
back to Dilghaut, and damn all the glory of
smashing the Rajah.

KYNASTON (*almost speechless, waves him to go*).
No — no — go — go ——

> (CARNAC *shakes hands with him very
> warmly, and then hurries off* L., *leav-
> ing group gathered around* KYNASTON.
> *Scene is darkened and drawn up, and
> discovers Scene III.*)

SCENE III

THE ROAD IN FRONT OF OLIVE ARNISON'S BUNGALOW

The bungalow is to the L. *of the stage, and takes up about three-quarters of the stage at back, showing a view of an Indian city to the* R. *at back. Creepers in front of the bungalow. There is a veranda running all around the bungalow, approached by some five or six steps. Time : Dawn. The dawn is magenta in India. The sun rises throughout the scene until it is full day.*

Discover OLIVE *on veranda in a handsome dressing-gown, watching, looking off very intently,* R., *the first rays of the rising sun striking her face.*

OLIVE (*looking off very earnestly*). You're late, sir! Make haste, or Colonel Carnac will be here before you. (*Listens intently, leaning towards* R. *Calls.*) Ayah! (AYAH *appears at window.*) Hark! Do you hear anything ?

AYAH. No, Memsahib. There is nothing.

OLIVE. Yes! Drums! They're coming back! Go and fetch my new pink morning dress. No. Stay! The little blue silk with the lace. Make haste! No, Ayah! I shall look best in white. Bring me the new white gown with the golden girdle and the little toy daggers.

(*Military music very, very faintly heard in the distance.*)

Enter BARTON, R., *below.*

OLIVE (*calls down*). Ah, Dicky! how has it gone?

BARTON. Splendidly! We've smashed them into smithereens, and Syrett has got the Rajah and all his suite.

OLIVE. Prisoners?

BARTON. Yes. (*She claps her hands.*) He's bringing them on here.

OLIVE. Here? (*To* AYAH.) My dress! My dress! Be quick! (*Walking backwards and forwards in great excitement, calling down to* BARTON.) Yes, go on! Tell me!

BARTON. He sent me on to know if you and all the ladies are safe.

OLIVE. Yes, all except Lady Scrivener. Some stragglers came up in the middle of the night and shot her on her veranda.

BARTON. Good heavens! Lady Scrivener wounded! Not dangerously?

OLIVE. Yes, I fear.

AYAH (*at window with a very pretty white dress*). The Memsahib's dress.

OLIVE. I must change my dress. (*Going into window, calling to him.*) Tell me some more about the fighting. Who has done anything?

BARTON. Syrett fought like a fiend. They got us into a corner once, just as it was growing dusk. But Syrett rallied us and drove them into the river. We drowned a few hundred and bayonetted the rest.

OLIVE. Is Colonel Syrett wounded?

BARTON. No, as good luck would have it.

OLIVE. Not wounded. (*With a shade of disappointment. To* AYAH.) Make haste! Make haste, creature! Don't you hear the music? Don't go, Dicky! Tell me some more!

BARTON. I must go and ask for Lady Scrivener. Colonel Syrett told me to tell you that he is bringing the Rajah and all his prisoners along this road.   (*Exit* BARTON, R.)

OLIVE. Along this road! (*To* AYAH.) Clumsy! I'll dress myself.

> (*Runs out, arranging her dress as she goes along. Music growing nearer. Enter down below,* L., CARNAC, *haggard, tired, broken down with fatigue. Music nearer, and* OLIVE *begins dancing and humming, and clapping her hands in great excitement.* CARNAC *calls out to her from below.*)

CARNAC.   Mrs. Arnison!

OLIVE (*carelessly*).   Oh, it's you!   (*Turns again towards the music.*)   What has kept you all night?

CARNAC.   We found the Nawab in greater force than we expected.   It took us till dusk to clear him out of the villages.   Then we couldn't get on the traces of the English ladies.   They are all missing except Miss Ford and her Ayah.   It was eight o'clock before I got away.   Then I lost my way in the dark, my horse broke his leg in a hole, and I've had to drag on here on foot.

OLIVE (*carelessly*).   How unfortunate!

CARNAC.   What has happened here?   Has Syrett attacked the Rajah?

OLIVE.   Yes.   A splendid engagement.   And I saw the fighting.   It was all round here last evening.   Syrett has taken the Rajah prisoner, and is bringing him home with all his suite!   Look, they're just turning the corner.

> (*Music growing nearer, she throws up her arms.*)

CARNAC (*calls out*).   Mrs. Arnison!   Olive!   I want to speak to you.

OLIVE.   Not now.   By-and-by.

CARNAC.   Won't you speak to me?

OLIVE (*smiling down to him*).   When I've congratulated Colonel Syrett.

CARNAC.   Why didn't Colonel Syrett send you to Barat?

OLIVE.   Because he thought it would be best for us to stay here.

> (*She waves her handkerchief off, dancing and humming with the music.* CARNAC *stretches out his arms towards her with a gesture of despair, and then goes wearily to the veranda steps and sits upon them.*)

Enter RADNAGE, R.

CARNAC.   Oh, Billy, where are you going.

RADNAGE.   To get the hospital ready, sir.

CARNAC.   Have you got many cases?

RADNAGE.   Not a great many, considering. You've heard about Lady Scrivener?

CARNAC.   No.   What?

RADNAGE.   Badly wounded.

CARNAC.   Not dangerously?

RADNAGE.   Hum!   She won't die, but she'll be a lame old dicky bird for the rest of her life.

CARNAC.   Good heavens!   What will the General say?

RADNAGE (*pointing up to* OLIVE).   That it's a blanked silly trick to have a parcel of women buzzing around you when there's any fighting to do.

CARNAC. Get through your hospital cases as soon as you can. Then ride over to Fyzapore. Find out Ford. Major Kynaston is with him, badly wounded. Billy, I'm afraid it's all over with him.

RADNAGE. Poor old psalm-singer. Well, after all, he's the only one of us that's in anything like prime Christmas condition for going aloft.

CARNAC. Stick to him to the very last, and pull him through if you can.

> (*Looks up at* OLIVE, *who is still leaning over the balcony, waving handkerchief with great excitement.*)

RADNAGE (*comes up to* CARNAC). Carnac old fellow.   (*Glancing up at* OLIVE.)

CARNAC (*not turning round, still looking at* OLIVE). Well?

RADNAGE (*pointing at* OLIVE). For heaven's sake, Carnac, don't let there be another such a damned fool as myself on this terrestrial sphere.

CARNAC (*still looking up at* OLIVE). Get away to your hospital—and then on to Kynaston! Quick!

RADNAGE. I'm off. (*Goes to extreme* L., *looks at* CARNAC, *shrugs his shoulders.*) Adieu, twin

spiritual brother.   We shall meet at the bottom
of the slope.

> (*Exit* L. *Music swells louder and louder.
> Enter a mixed crowd of natives and
> English, cheering. Enter* SYRETT *with
> immense pride and excitement of vic-
> tory. He is followed by the* MAHARA-
> JAH OF MOTIALA *and his suite, prison-
> ers in the charge of* BARTON. OLIVE
> waves her hand to* SYRETT, *who bows
> to her.* CARNAC *has mounted the
> veranda steps and is behind the foliage,
> watching jealously.* OLIVE *runs quickly
> down the steps.* CARNAC *intercepts
> her for a moment, and then allows her
> to pass. She runs down the steps to*
> SYRETT, CARNAC *remaining above
> them.* SYRETT *affects not to see*
> CARNAC.)

OLIVE.   You've returned, and victorious?

SYRETT (*pointing to prisoners*).   As you see.

OLIVE.   But not wounded?

SYRETT.   Luckily—no.

OLIVE.   Luckily—no.

> (CARNAC *comes down to them.*)

SYRETT (*salutes. His manner throughout the
scene is one of great politeness to* CARNAC, *covering the most insolent intention*).   I beg pardon,
sir. I did not notice you. After you had gone

✳

yesterday, Captain Bell brought the information that the Rajah was in great force at Blakepore. I was somewhat at a loss to know what to do, but I considered it advisable to attack him at once. I hope you approve of my action.

CARNAC. Go on.

SYRETT. We were repulsed at first and driven back on the cantonments with some loss. But I succeeded in rallying my men, and about six last evening I drove the Rajah back upon the river and utterly routed him. I pursued through the night and succeeded in taking him and all his suite prisoners. I have the honour to hand you over my prisoners.

(*Courteous bow and salaam exchanged between* CARNAC *and the* RAJAH.)

CARNAC. Mr. Barton, his Highness and his suite are in your charge. You will place him and them in the large unoccupied bungalow near mine, and put a guard over them. I need not tell you to treat his Highness with every courtesy.

BARTON. Yes, sir.

CARNAC (*to* RAJAH). I will arrange to see your Highness this afternoon.

RAJAH. It will not be necessary, Sahib.

CARNAC. I will then tell you what arrangements I have been able to make for your Highness's safety and comfort.

RAJAH.   It will not be necessary, Sahib.

CARNAC.   I think it will be necessary, your Highness.

> (*Motions to* BARTON *to take the* RAJAH *and his suite off. Exeunt the* RAJAH *and his suite in charge of soldiers. Exit* BARTON *after the* RAJAH, *people moving off, cheering.*)

SYRETT (*to* CARNAC).   I have the honour to present you, sir, with the swords of my prisoners (*with great mock humility*), or, I should say, *your* prisoners.

> (CAPTAIN BELL *comes forward with swords and presents them to* CARNAC.)

CARNAC.   Take them to my office, Captain Bell.

BELL.   Yes, sir.   (*Exit* BELL, *with swords.*)

SYRETT.   I regret to report Captain Baynes and twenty men killed, Mr. Lewis and Mr. Darrell and thirty men wounded and missing. Lady Scrivener was shot on her veranda by some stragglers.

CARNAC.   Why didn't you send the ladies to Barat as I directed?

SYRETT.   I considered, sir, it was judicious to keep them here.   I hope you approve of my decision.

CARNAC.   Why didn't you send me a message?

SYRETT.   I did, sir.

CARNAC.   At what time?

SYRETT.   About six, sir.

CARNAC.   Why didn't you send before?

SYRETT (*with a sneer*).   I considered it judicious to wait, sir, until I was sure of victory. You didn't receive my message?

CARNAC.   No.

SYRETT.   I'm sorry, sir, we were deprived of the great advantage of your presence. Doubtless you would have been glad to lead us. I hope, sir, you approve of my conduct?

CARNAC.   I shall need your assistance in preparing the report for headquarters. Please go to my office. I will come to you there.

SYRETT (*with great insolence*).   I hope you approve of my conduct, sir?

(CARNAC *does not reply.*)

OLIVE.   Let me offer you my congratulations, and I'm sure you must be hungry. My servants have just prepared my choti-hazri. May I offer you my hospitality?

SYRETT.   Thank you. I am very hungry.

OLIVE.   This way.

CARNAC (*to* SYRETT).   Meet me at my office to prepare the report in half an hour.

SYRETT.   I fear, sir, I may be a little longer.

CARNAC (*in a deadly rage*).   Meet me at my office in half an hour, sir,

SYRETT (*with great insolence*). I will do my best, sir, but I fear I may be a little longer.

OLIVE (*smiling*). Will you please allow us to pass, Colonel Carnac?

(*He steps politely aside, and they go up. As she passes into bungalow she gives* SYRETT *the rose she has been wearing.*)

CARNAC (*in deadly rage, goes a step or two up the steps, comes down, rages up and down the stage, madly*). Was ever such cursed, cursed, hellish luck, and all to save that slip of a girl. If it hadn't been for her I should have done it! Was ever such damned luck in this world?

Enter, R., ELLICE *and* AMINA, *very much fatigued, in charge of* LOVATT. ELLICE *is dragging on* AMINA'S *arm.*

CARNAC (*carelessly*). Oh, so you've got here?

ELLICE. Yes, thanks again to you. We should have been killed by those men if you hadn't stayed with us.

CARNAC (*taking no notice of her*). Mr. Lovatt, Lady Scrivener is wounded, and I fear won't be able to receive Miss Ford.

LOVATT. Miss Ford is very much fatigued, sir. She nearly fainted several times on the way.

CARNAC. Well, make haste and get her into some lady's care. (*To* ELLICE, *a little impatiently.*) Now, Miss Ford, you must please bear up until Mr. Lovatt can get someone to take care of you.

ELLICE (*very much hurt at his careless manner*). Thank you, Colonel Carnac. (*He turns away towards the bungalow.*) Won't you even let me thank you for all you've done for me ?

CARNAC (*still coldly*). Oh, there's no need for that. (*Looking intently at bungalow. She looks at him with the utmost reproach, staggers a step or two after* LOVATT, *and then falls into* CARNAC'S *arms in a faint. He sustains her, looks at her.*) Mr. Lovatt, go to my bearer, tell him to take all my traps into my office and to prepare my bungalow for Miss Ford and her Ayah for the present. Then go to Mrs. Carmichael and ask her to be kind enough to receive Miss Ford.

LOVATT. Yes, sir.

> (CARNAC, *very tenderly, takes his pocket flask, forces some of its contents down her lips, she revives, looks at him.*)

ELLICE. Is it you ? I'm so sorry I fainted. Where am I to go?

CARNAC. If you will accept my bungalow for an hour or two, I shall be delighted.

ELLICE. Oh, but I've been so much trouble to you already ! Forgive me !

CARNAC.   Forgive *me* for being so rude to you just now.

ELLICE (*struggling towards* AMINA).   Ayah, help me.

CARNAC.   No, take my arm. I'll see you over to my bungalow. That's better.

ELLICE.   How good you are to me.

> (*A little laugh from* OLIVE *is heard from bungalow.* CARNAC *turns jealously round, hesitates for a moment or two.*)

CARNAC.   Mr. Lovatt, will you kindly take Miss Ford to my bungalow? I'll be there shortly.

> (LOVATT *takes* ELLICE *off,* R.; *she looks round at* CARNAC *as she goes off.* CARNAC *creeps jealously up the steps. A louder laugh from* OLIVE. CARNAC'S *hand seizes the shrub growing by the steps and crushes its leaves.*)

CURTAIN.

(*A fortnight passes between Acts I and II.*)

E

ACT II

*Club with veranda runs all along the R. side of the
stage, and is brilliantly lighted up. At the back a
great river shaded with palms, giving a view of
the opposite bank with a large ghaut or bathing-
place, marble palaces, and gardens, giving the impression of a decayed Indian city of some impor-
tance. On the L., down stage, a little pavilion.
Seats, chairs and tables, and different places as
required. The time is night, after dinner. As curtain goes up groups of English people in evening
dress are walking and seated about the grounds
taking coffee, etc., waited upon by Indian servants.
The Englishmen are in the white Indian evening
dress. Towards the front of the stage are* LOVATT,
BELL *and* MRS. CARMICHAEL.

MRS. CARMICHAEL. So the General has
arrived.

BELL. Yes. Of course he's dining at
home with Lady Scrivener, but he's going to
look round here by-and-by.

Mrs. Car. I hear he's very angry about Lady Scrivener's wound.

Bell. Yes. You ladies ought to have been sent to Barat.

Lovatt. The General's going to make a thorough inquiry into that as soon as he meets Carnac.   (*Goes and looks in Club window.*)

Enter Barton *from the Club. Comes up to them.*

Mrs. Car. Is Colonel Carnac still in the dining-room.

Barton. Yes.

Mrs. Car. Did you notice that he dined by himself ?

Barton. Did he ?

Mrs. Car. In a corner, and had a whole bottle of champagne.

Bell. And a liqueur or two after.

Barton. What's that to Carnac ? He'll carry it, and be as fresh as paint if he's called out at four o'clock to-morrow morning.

Olive *enters unnoticed behind them in beautiful evening dress.*

Bell. Carnac hasn't been quite himself the last week or two.

Mrs. Car. I suppose we may put that down to Mrs. Arnison. I wish her husband would come and take her away.

Olive (*who has overheard*). Oh, my dear Mrs. Carmichael, my husband is far too busy looking after somebody else's wife to be able to pay much attention to me. But, dear man, he has done his best under the circumstances. He has sent his sister to mount guard over me. (*Smiling sweetly all round.*) Did you notice that woman with the straw-coloured hair dining with me and Colonel Syrett? That's Mrs. Remington, my husband's sister.

Mrs. Car. (*a little confused*). I only thought —that—that while your husband is away you might be a little——

Olive. Dull? Lonely? Not at all! While Mrs. Remington is here I am as happy and merry as if I were cloistered. Dear Laura! She never allows me to feel lonely for a moment. Here she is. Watch!

Mrs. Remington *enters from Club down stage. Exit* Olive *very slowly in rapt and pious contemplation of the stars. Enter* Colonel Syrett *from Club up stage. He is sauntering after* Olive, l., *when* Mrs. Remington *goes very quickly after* Olive, *calling out as she goes.*

MRS. REMINGTON. Olive, dearest, isn't this your fan?

> (SYRETT *saunters slowly after them.*
> *Dance music begins in Club.*)

BARTON (*looking off* L. *after* SYRETT *and* OLIVE). I haven't a fraction of curiosity in my composition, and I never breathe a word of scandal, but I'd give my next year's pay to know ——

BELL. What, Dicky?

BARTON (*very markedly*). Whether there really is anything between Syrett and Mrs. Arnison.

Enter CARNAC *from Club. He looks anxiously round as if searching for someone. He is a little flushed, his eyes are bright, but he is not noticeably intoxicated. His left arm hangs at his side, and his left breast is bandaged under his evening dress. They look at him.* LOVATT *is seen to go and offer his arm to* EVA CAR- MICHAEL, *who is on the steps.*

BELL (*to* MRS. CARMICHAEL). Our dance, Mrs. Carmichael.

> (*Offering his arm. They all go off into*
> *Club, leaving* BARTON *and* CARNAC.)

BARTON. Have you seen the General, sir?

CARNAC. Yes, Dicky.

BARTON. I suppose he'll ask me why Lady Scrivener and the ladies were not sent on to Barat.

CARNAC. If he does you will tell him the truth, that Colonel Syrett was short of men, and judged it better not to spare you. And you'll be careful to convey that no blame attaches to Colonel Syrett.

BARTON. Yes, sir.

(*Exit into Club. Left alone, COLONEL CARNAC goes L., looks off, shows rage, anguish, unconsciously helps himself to liquor left on the table, walks up and down the stage with rage, looks off L. SYRETT saunters on, L., the two men look at each other. SYRETT sits down. Silence for some moments.*)

The following scene must be played with great intensity and excitement by both CARNAC and SYRETT. In the earlier part CARNAC, who has been drinking freely at dinner, is possessed by jealous rage and fear that SYRETT is the lover of OLIVE. When OLIVE enters, CARNAC makes one last effort to dominate her by the reckless force of his passion. He succeeds, and in the flush of victory is insolently triumphant towards SYRETT. SYRETT, on the other hand, is at first cool and insolent, but when he realizes that he is losing

OLIVE, *he in his turn becomes mad with jealousy, and, piqued by* CARNAC'S *behaviour, is ready in his desperation to listen to the suggestions of* MAHOMET. *It is a situation where the essential passions of men should be shown rather than their ordinary behaviour. If this jealous rage on the part of both men, a rage overruling for the time all other considerations, is not shown by the actors, the significance of the scene will be lost, and it will seem to the audience impolite or colourless. And further, the succeeding scenes between* SYRETT *and* MAHOMET *will appear to be unnatural and without foundation.*

CARNAC (*at length*).   Arthur!

SYRETT.   Well?

CARNAC.   If duelling were allowed I would find some pretext to challenge you, and I think I should kill you.

SYRETT.   Possibly.   Possibly I might kill you.

CARNAC.   I *know* that you might have called me back to lead the attack a fortnight ago.   I *know* that you kept Barton from taking the ladies to Barat because a lady asked you.

SYRETT.   Quite true.

CARNAC.   I've been asking myself all the day whether I should tell the General the truth and get you court-martialled as you deserve.

SYRETT.   And you've told him?

CARNAC. No. I held my tongue and shielded you because——

SYRETT. Because?

CARNAC. Because — well, because I can afford to. So I shielded you.

SYRETT. Thank you.

CARNAC. Now tell me one thing.

SYRETT. Go on.

CARNAC. We promised to fight fair.

SYRETT. We did.

CARNAC (*comes up to him, in a whisper*). Is the fight over? Have I lost?

(SYRETT *smiles but does not answer.*)

CARNAC. Do you hear? Have I lost?

SYRETT. My dear Stacey, suppose for sake of argument that you had lost, to tell you so would be to play the traitor to a lady.

CARNAC. No. You know me. A woman's reputation is sacred to me. I fight fair. If you have won, I leave the field. (*Same whisper.*) Have I lost?

SYRETT (*with the same inscrutable smile*). What would you have me say under the circumstances?

CARNAC. Tell me the truth. Have I lost?

SYRETT (*still smiling*). My dear Stacey, you may guess what infinite satisfaction it gives me to assure you that you have —— not — lost!

Enter OLIVE. CARNAC *looks steadfastly at him,
looks at her.   All through following scenes, he
keenly watches their manner to see if they be-
tray any secret relationship.*

OLIVE. What's the matter? You are not
quarrelling again?

CARNAC. No. I was just raising a little
question with Arthur.

SYRETT. Mrs. Arnison, I think this is our
dance.

> (*Offering arm.*   OLIVE *barely takes it.*
> SYRETT *makes a movement to go into
> the Club.*)

CARNAC (*politely intercepting them*). One
moment, Arthur. Mrs. Arnison could settle
this little question between us.

SYRETT. By-and-by, Stacey. Mrs. Arnison
is engaged to me for this dance.

> (*Trying to get* OLIVE *into Club.*)

CARNAC. But if Mrs. Arnison prefers to
stay. (*Covertly pulling her wrap from her shoulders.*) Pardon me, your wrap is slipping —
allow me!

> (*About to put* OLIVE's *wrap on her shoul-
> der with his right arm.*)

SYRETT. No, allow me!

> (*They both try to put her wrap on, but
> CARNAC snatches the wrap.*)

CARNAC.   Mrs. Arnison shall decide.

OLIVE (*looks from one to the other, then to* SYRETT).   You are to have the dance.   Colonel Carnac shall put on my cloak.

(SYRETT *shows great mortification.*)

CARNAC.   Get away, you lucky rascal.   Let me do all the work; you shall have all the smiles.

(*Drawing on the wrap with his one arm.*)

OLIVE.   Only one arm, Colonel Carnac?

CARNAC.   It's enough for fighting, loving (*very tenderly adjusting wrap*), and playing the ladies' maid.

OLIVE.   But what's the matter with that?

(*Pointing to his left arm.*)

CARNAC.   Got a slash this afternoon, right across this arm and my left breast.

OLIVE.   Wounded?   Why haven't I heard of it?

CARNAC.   Because I haven't mentioned it.

OLIVE (*very much interested and concerned*). But it's deep — look!   (*Pointing to a little mark which has just appeared on his shirt front.*) It's bleeding now!

CARNAC.   It's nothing.

SYRETT (*to* OLIVE).   I think we ought to be taking our places.

OLIVE.   One moment!   (*To* CARNAC.)   You must go and get your wound dressed at once.

CARNAC. Oh, Burgess has bandaged it, and
I'll get Billy Radnage to look to it when he
comes back from Fyzapore.

OLIVE (*sympathetically*). I'm so sorry.

SYRETT. Mrs. Arnison, may I?

(*Offering arm a little impatiently.*)

OLIVE. Oh, one moment, if you please,
Colonel Syrett. (*To* CARNAC.) How did you
get that wound?

CARNAC. I went to do a little reconnoitring this afternoon. As I was riding back I
fell in with a troop of stragglers. They cut
me off from my party and got me into a
tight place. This is the result. I've lost a
pint or two of blood, but I've drunk a bottle
or two of wine. And now I'm ready to try
conclusions with a few more natives, or with
my friend Arthur, or with you.

OLIVE. Oh, what conclusions could you
try with me?

SYRETT (*impatiently*). We shall miss our dance.

OLIVE. Will that matter?

SYRETT. Very much to me.

CARNAC. Very well, then, go and dance it,
my dear Arthur, and leave Mrs. Arnison with
me to settle this little question.

OLIVE. Ah, this little question! What is
it? (*To* SYRETT.) Would you very much
mind if I stayed out this dance?

SYRETT (*deeply mortified*).   If you please.

OLIVE.   Look at that charming little seat, just made for three ! Shall we go and sit there ? And all be good friends ?

CARNAC.   By all means.   Let us be the best of friends, eh, Arthur ? You're looking glum ! What's the matter ?

SYRETT.   Nothing.

OLIVE.   How unlucky to get wounded ?

CARNAC.   Arthur is the lucky man of us two, aren't you, Arthur ?

SYRETT (*with meaning*).   Yes, I am, Stacey.

CARNAC (*looks at him, looks at* OLIVE).   So you say, Arthur.   So you say.

SYRETT.   You don't believe me ?

CARNAC.   If Mrs. Arnison says so.

OLIVE.   How is it you always begin to quarrel in my presence ? What is this little question I am to settle ?

CARNAC.   Why that is the very question — who is the lucky man of us two, Arthur or I ?

OLIVE.   Oh, how can I say ! Colonel Syrett was very lucky to take the Rajah a fortnight ago.

CARNAC.   Yes, just as my back was turned, eh, Arthur ? I hadn't left the lines.   You ought to have called me back, Arthur.

SYRETT.   I did as I thought best.

CARNAC. I shouldn't have done it if I'd been you, Arthur. It was a little bit sharp practice, a tiny little bit off the square, eh, Arthur?

SYRETT. Do you accuse me of acting dishonourably?

CARNAC. Not at all, my dear fellow. Only as a man of honour I shouldn't have done it myself. Especially after our agreement.

OLIVE. Agreement? What agreement?

CARNAC. Arthur and I have a little friendly agreement.

OLIVE. About what?

CARNAC. About a woman.

OLIVE. A friendly agreement about a woman! How strange! Now if it had been a disagreement——

CARNAC. Ah, that is what ordinary men do for ordinary women. They quarrel. But for the most extraordinary woman that walks this earth Arthur and I did not quarrel, did we, Arthur? We agreed that the best man should win.

OLIVE. And did the best man win?

CARNAC (*looks full in her face*). Did he? Did he? Is she won? Tell me the truth. Is she won?

OLIVE (*startled, looks from one to the other, then looks full at* SYRETT, *and says to* CARNAC). No. You can believe that or not, as you choose, but it's true.

CARNAC (*to* SYRETT). Arthur, my dear boy (*points with his thumb over his shoulder to the Club*), you've lost that dance!

SYRETT (*going* L., *calls off*). What are you doing there?

Enter L., MAHOMET ALI, *salaams.*

MAHOMET. You told me to wait for you, Sahib, with the boat.

SYRETT. You needn't wait. I'll drive back.

(MAHOMET *salaams and exit.* SYRETT
comes up again to OLIVE *and* CARNAC.
Is about to sit down again on the seat.)

CARNAC. Going to join our little party again, Arthur?

SYRETT. No. (*Maddened, to* CARNAC.) I want to speak to you alone. Do you hear, alone! (CARNAC *jumps up, and* MRS. ARNISON
steps in between them.)

OLIVE. Oh please! Please! Will you control yourselves? People are coming! Colonel Carnac, if you please.

CARNAC (*offering his arm*). Will you give me this next dance?

SYRETT. Mrs. Arnison, I think you owe me a dance.

CARNAC. Will you give me this next dance?

OLIVE. Can you dance with that arm?

CARNAC. Will you try me for a partner?

(*She gives him her arm, and they go
towards Club.*)

CARNAC. And you know my little friendly
agreement with Arthur. The best man is to
win. If it came to wagering a trifle—a pair
of gloves, or say that rose you wear—would
you bet on Arthur or me?

SYRETT (*with desperate energy*). Mrs. Arnison, give me that rose.

CARNAC (*to* OLIVE). Would you bet on
Arthur or me?

OLIVE (*takes rose, looks from one to the other*).
I would bet on you!

(*Giving the rose to* CARNAC.)

CARNAC. Arthur, my dear boy, you've lost
that rose.

(*Exit into Club with* OLIVE *on his arm.
SYRETT left alone, goes up to the Club
windows, looks in at the dancing.
MAHOMET enters stealthily from behind
pavilion, L. SYRETT comes back from
the Club; with a furious gesture, stands
centre, maddened with jealous rage;
looks up, sees* MAHOMET *standing
against pavilion.* MAHOMET *salaams.*)

SYRETT. Have you been there all the while?

MAHOMET. Yes, Sahib.

SYRETT. I sha'n't want you again to-night.

MAHOMET (*salaams and comes up to him. Very slowly and with great suggestion*). If the Sahib should have any private commands——

SYRETT. About what?

MAHOMET. About Carnac Sahib——

SYRETT. What do you mean?

MAHOMET. My father served the noble Englefield Sahib. There was a very beautiful Memsahib — Englefield Sahib loved her very much.

SYRETT. Well?

MAHOMET. The Memsahib's husband was a beast, a pig. The Englefield Sahib hated him, as you, Sahib, hate Carnac Sahib.

SYRETT. Well?

MAHOMET. The husband died.

SYRETT. Well?

MAHOMET. The husband died.

SYRETT (*looks at him*). You blackguard! How dare you breathe such a thing to me!

MAHOMET (*unruffled, salaams*). I am sorry I spoke, Sahib. The husband died. It was strange how he died.

SYRETT. Get back to the bungalow and wait for me.

> (MAHOMET *salaams and goes* L. *to pavilion, but does not go off, watches* SYRETT, *who goes to Club windows and looks in.* SYRETT *again shows rage of jealousy.*)

Enter OLIVE, *runs down Club steps towards* L.
CARNAC *is following her.*

SYRETT (*beside himself with jealousy*).   Mrs.
Arnison, may I beg this dance ?

OLIVE.   Oh, I fear I can't.   I've saddled
poor dear Lord Darlow with my husband's
sister in the pavilion yonder, and I must go
and relieve her.   (*Going off* L.)

SYRETT (*to* OLIVE).   Give me one dance to-
night ?

OLIVE.   I can't promise.

SYRETT (*beside himself with jealous rage*).   Give
me one dance to-night !
          (*Putting himself in front of her, stopping
          her exit.*)

OLIVE.   I can't.   I think you are rather
rude to me.

SYRETT (*mad with jealousy, stopping her*).   You
have to drive home.   Let me at least escort
you and Mrs. Remington to your bungalow.

OLIVE.   I have promised Colonel Carnac.
                              (*Exit* L.)

CARNAC (*looks at him*).   Ah !   That's how I
felt, Arthur, a fortnight ago when you took my
command away from me.   (*Exit after* OLIVE.)

MAHOMET (*has stood very calmly all the while.
He now comes up to* SYRETT).   Has the Sahib
any commands ?   (SYRETT *looks at him.*)

F

Enter AMINA, *up stage*, R., *unobserved.*

MAHOMET. Has the Sahib any commands?
(SYRETT *does not speak.*) The pig of the husband died this way: the Memsahib had some
jewels, and some thieves came to steal them.
There was fighting in the dark, and in the fighting the husband was killed. (SYRETT *looks at
him.*) But there are many ways that people
die. A Sahib at Delhi died of a snake-bite,
another Sahib died of sunstroke—so many ways
there are that Sahibs die, and there is no talk.
If an English Sahib goes to that Memsahib's
bungalow to-night—to steal her jewels—or to-
morrow night—or any night—I know a faithful
servant at Memsahib's, and we will provide that
the thief shall not come away with his life.

SYRETT (*looks at him a moment*). I sha'n't
want your services to-night, or any night, at any
time that you think Mrs. Arnison's jewels are in
danger.

MAHOMET. The Sahib's commands shall be
obeyed. And the Sahib need have no fear. It
will be an accident. And there will be no
talk.
                (*The two men exchange looks. Exit
                SYRETT into Club. MAHOMET goes,
                looks* L., AMINA *comes up to him.*)
AMINA. Is it Carnac Sahib that will come

like a thief in the night to steal the Memsahib's jewels?

MAHOMET. Carnac Sahib a thief! What strange thing is this, my sister?

> (MAHOMET *is going off* L., AMINA *is following; he turns round.*)

MAHOMET. Go now to your Memsahib, and follow me not!

AMINA. You will do no harm to Carnac Sahib?

MAHOMET. Why, then, should I do him harm? Put these evil thoughts from thy heart, my sister.   (*Exit* L.)

Enter ELLICE *from the Club with* EVA CARMI-CHAEL, *as if looking for someone.*

ELLICE. Wait a minute, Eva, I'm not sure whether I'm engaged for this dance.

AMINA. Are you looking for someone, Missie Sahib?

ELLICE. Colonel Carnac asked me yesterday for a dance? Have you seen him?

AMINA. He is there in the pavilion with the Arnison Memsahib and her sister.

> (*Pointing off* L.)

ELLICE (*looking off* L.). I daresay Colonel Carnac has forgotten me. No, he's coming! Who is that man following him?

AMINA.   It is my brother Mahomet.   He is bearer to Syrett Sahib.   (*Exit.*)

> (ELLICE *turns away very shyly as* CARNAC *enters rather excited.   He is going into Club, but happens to catch sight of her.*)

CARNAC.   Ah, my dear Miss Ford, how is it I've not seen you before?   You're quite comfortable, I hope, with Mrs. Carmichael?

ELLICE.   Oh yes, thank you.   It's kind of her to have me—a stranger.

CARNAC.   A stranger!   Oh no.   In times like this we English are all one family.

ELLICE.   When shall I be able to go back to Fyzapore to my father and sister?

CARNAC.   It wouldn't be safe yet, but I'll take any message you have.   I'm riding over to-morrow to see Major Kynaston.

ELLICE.   If it isn't safe for me it isn't safe for you.

CARNAC.   Oh, I take my chance.

ELLICE.   Can't I take mine?

CARNAC.   Risk a valuable young life like yours?

ELLICE.   Your life is far more valuable than mine, and yet you risk it.

CARNAC.   It's my business.

ELLICE.   To risk your life and save mine.

CARNAC.   Now tell me what message shall I take to Fyzapore?

ELLICE.   Only my dearest love to them both, and a kiss to May; you may kiss her, she's only eleven.

CARNAC.   I may kiss her; she's only eleven.

ELLICE.   And give her this flower — oh, you're wearing a flower.

CARNAC.   I'll take this too, and kiss the little maiden of eleven.   How is it you're not dancing ?

ELLICE.   I thought that—I mean yesterday, you ——

CARNAC.   What ?

ELLICE.   When you were at Mrs. Carmichael's ——

CARNAC (*remembering*).   Of course, I asked you for a dance.   And I forgot!   Forgive me.   The General has just sent for me, but I think there's time.   Are you engaged for the next ?

ELLICE.   No.

CARNAC.   Then will you give me the pleasure ——

(*She shows intense delight, takes his arm, and goes towards Club steps.*)

CARNAC.   Did I forget ?   Did I forget ?

ELLICE (*delighted*).   But you've remembered now.   (*They are going towards Club.*)

Enter from Club, GENERAL SIR HARDINGE SCRIV-
ENER, *a wiry, well-seasoned soldier, about sixty,
with a lot of medals.*

SCRIVENER.   Carnac, I want to speak to you.

CARNAC.   Yes, sir.   I was about to dance
with Miss Ford, but, of course, if it is important, sir——

SCRIVENER.   It is important, and as Lady
Scrivener is not quite so well to-night, perhaps
I may ask Miss Ford to excuse you.

ELLICE (*much disappointed*).   Oh yes, of
course.   (*Drops* CARNAC'S *arm.*)

CARNAC.   I'm so sorry, Miss Ford.   I must
beg a dance another time.

ELLICE.   Yes——

> (CARNAC *bows to her; she goes towards
> Club; meets* EVA CARMICHAEL, *who is
> coming out.*   CARNAC *goes to speak to*
> SCRIVENER.)

EVA.   What's the matter, darling?

> (ELLICE *bursts into tears on* EVA'S
> *shoulder.*)

EVA.   Never mind, dear!   Don't cry!   It will
all come right by-and-by.   (*Soothing her.*)

> (*Exeunt* ELLICE *and* EVA *into Club.
> The* GENERAL *and* CARNAC *have been
> talking.*)

SCRIVENER.   I am not at all satisfied that

Syrett is not very much to blame for not sending the ladies to Barat.   Candidly, what do
you think about it ?

CARNAC.   He says he acted for the best, sir.
I don't think you ought to go behind that.

SCRIVENER (*dissatisfied*).   H'm !   H'm !   I've
just had a telegram from Calcutta.   They leave
the Rajah in my hands.   I can either send him
there to be tried, or, if I think it advisable, I
can try him here by court-martial.

CARNAC.   Hadn't we better keep him here
for a little while, sir ?   I believe he is sending
messages to the Rajah of Sirhoot.

SCRIVENER.   That may mean a bigger job
on our hands than we've had yet.

CARNAC.   Yes, unless we can pump, or
squeeze, or frighten the whole truth out of him.

SCRIVENER.   Then you advise us to keep
him for a few days ?

CARNAC.   Yes.   I'll have him carefully
watched meantime.   Will you leave the matter in my hands, sir ?

SCRIVENER.   Very well, Carnac. (*Takes out
watch.*)   I must get back to Lady Scrivener.
Good-night.

CARNAC.   Good-night, sir.

> (*Exit into Club.*   CARNAC *goes a few steps
> as if going into Club, then turns towards
> L.*   RADNAGE'S *voice heard in the Club.*)

RADNAGE (*off*). Where? Where? I must see him at once. (*Enters from Club, in riding clothes, travel stained.*) Ah, Carnac!

CARNAC. Billy, what is it? How's Kynaston?

RADNAGE. Poor old psalm-singer!

CARNAC. Not dead?

RADNAGE. No, but he's tuning up for Paradise. He's been delirious all the afternoon, seeing cherubims, and demi-semi-quavering hallelujahs. This stony old heart hasn't been so much touched since my poor aunt played the church organ on Sundays, and I chirped out the Litany from a dirty surplice, and made eyes at the young ladies' school opposite. (*To* WAITER.) Khitmurgar! Brandy and soda. Quick!

CARNAC. Why did you let me leave him yesterday?

RADNAGE. Because I knew you were wanted here. If you want to see him alive you'd better ride over.

CARNAC. Of course I'll go to him at once.
                    (*Goes and looks off* L.)

RADNAGE. You'll find him in a very queer state.   (WAITER *brings brandy and soda.*)

CARNAC. How so?

RADNAGE. He's very anxious to make a family party of all his old chums, so that we can hold a perpetual sacred sing-song in the sweet by-and-by, beyond the river. And the said river running nothing but a teetotal liquid, just to please and poultice him, I took my davy I'd be a strict teetotaler from this time forth. (*Drinks brandy.*) So he's very happy about me. I've found salvation. Another brandy and soda, waiter. But your condition is perilous, and there's only one way to save you.

CARNAC. What's that?

RADNAGE. You were engaged to his dead sister, weren't you?

CARNAC. Yes, fifteen years ago.

RADNAGE. He has been seeing her — Enid, isn't her name? — all the afternoon.

CARNAC. Where?

RADNAGE. In the course of constant ten-minute trips between his old home at Broad-stairs, the New Jerusalem, and this inferno of India. His one fixed idea is to see you before he dies, marry you to his sister, and get you safely boxed up with himself, and her, and me, in his family Paradise. And he won't die peaceably till he has done it.

CARNAC (*glancing off* L.). Of course I'll go to him at once. (*Looking off at* OLIVE.)

RADNAGE (*comes to him*). Carnac, old fellow——

CARNAC. Well?

RADNAGE. In spite of having old psalm-singer to propose me for the celestial club, I'm safe to get blackballed when the day of election comes.

CARNAC. Me too, Billy, me too!

(*Looking off* L.)

RADNAGE. No! No! I'm past praying for, but you aren't! Take a fool's advice! Ride over to Kynaston and let him box you up in his family Paradise and save you from a woman who will else be your damnation as surely — as surely (*drinking*) as brandy will be mine! (*A very lively dance is struck up in the Club.*)

HOBBS (*enters very excitedly down stage,* R.). Carnac!

CARNAC. Padri!

RADNAGE. You haven't left Kynaston?

HOBBS. No. As soon as you had gone, he demanded to be brought here to see Colonel Carnac. I tried to quiet him, but he raved, and begged and prayed, so at last, just to soothe him, I got him on a litter and started. I thought we should meet Colonel Carnac on the way. You said you would send him.

RADNAGE. I've only just got here. I — (*ashamed*) I was detained on the way.

HOBBS (*contemptuously*). I might have known you would be detained on the way.

CARNAC. Where is Kynaston now?

HOBBS. I've got him just outside. He wanted to be brought in here, but I didn't like ——

KYNASTON (*voice off* R.). Make haste! Make haste! Take me to him! Quick!

 (*He is brought on down stage,* R., *on a litter.*)

CARNAC. Hedley, my dear old fellow, what is this? (*Calls out to Club.*) Stop that music!

KYNASTON. I couldn't die till I'd seen you! Stacey, I must save you from that woman before I die! I've been talking to Enid — (*looking round.*) Where is she? Enid! Enid! Don't leave me! She was here just now!

CARNAC. All right, old fellow, I'll send for her! (*Calls out.*) Stop that music, I say!

KYNASTON. Stacey, promise me one thing before I die!

CARNAC. What is it?

KYNASTON. Give up that woman, or be lost for ever!

CARNAC. Yes, yes, old fellow! Don't trouble about me!

KYNASTON. Give up that woman, or be lost for ever! (CARNAC *is silent.*) Give up that woman, or be lost for ever!

Hobbs. He's dying! Won't you promise him?

Carnac. I won't tell a lie to a dying man!

Ellice *enters quickly from Club, followed by other guests; the music suddenly stops; guests rush on and crowd round.*

Kynaston. Give her up, I say! Give her up, or —— (*Sees* Ellice.) Ah, Enid! Enid! (*Stretching out his hands to her.*) I'm so glad you've come!

Ellice (*to* Carnac). What does he mean?

Carnac. He's delirious! He thinks you are his sister!

Kynaston. Enid, come to me, dear!

Carnac. Don't cross him! He's dying!
(*She goes to him.*)

Kynaston. I want Stacey to promise to marry you, dear! And I know you love him! Stacey, it's my last wish! Let me know before I die that you're safe! Don't refuse me! (*To* Ellice.) Give him your hand, dear!
(Hobbs *makes an appealing gesture to* Carnac.)

Carnac (*to* Hobbs). To soothe him. I mean no more (*to* Ellice). It's only a dying man's fancy. Do you mind?
(*She gives* Carnac *her hand.*)

KYNASTON (*looks at them a moment*).   There !
There ! (*Sinks.*)   Thanks ! Thanks !   You're
safe now, Stacey !   I'm very happy !   I'm very
happy ! (*Dies.*)

> (CARNAC *bends over him, covers him with
> his cloak.* ELLICE *covers her face with
> her hands.*)

CURTAIN.

ACT III

Scene I

Front Scene to Set in Front of Scene II. Room in Colonel Carnac's Bungalow, showing the interior of the bungalow, whose exterior is shown in Act I, Scene I.

A large window at back showing the veranda outside, with sun-blinds drawn down to shut out back view. A door, R. A door, L. Time, morning.

Discover Carnac seated, smoking, at a table with a heap of military papers in front of him. There are other indications that the room is used temporarily as an office.

Carnac's *bearer*, Ali Kahn, *enters,* L., *showing in* Olive. Carnac *rises with great surprise and delight, throws away his cigar.* Olive *signs silence. Exit* Ali Kahn, L.

Carnac. You!
Olive. Yes.
Carnac (*under his breath*). I'm delighted.

(78)

OLIVE (*looks keenly at him*). Are you? What has been the matter with you the last ten days?

CARNAC. The death of my old friend Kynaston. It made me feel rather sad ——

OLIVE. And very virtuous?

CARNAC. I had a few virtuous qualms for three or four days.

OLIVE. For three or four days?

CARNAC. No healthy man allows his conscience to torture him for longer than that. Poor Hedley! And it was hard on the girl.

OLIVE. My friend, those virtuous qualms are still lingering about your conscience.

CARNAC. What, in your presence! Whew! (*Makes an action of blowing them away.*) They're gone.

OLIVE. I'm glad, because ——

CARNAC. Yes ——.

OLIVE. I have some news for you.

CARNAC. Tell me quickly. I expect the General.

OLIVE. The General!

CARNAC. He hasn't been able to move the office back to his bungalow on account of Lady Scrivener's illness. So we transact all the business here. Tell me the news quickly.

OLIVE (*significantly*). Mrs. Remington is ill.

CARNAC. Seriously ?

OLIVE. Seriously, poor angel. I'm afraid she must keep her room for a day or two.

CARNAC. Then——?

> (OLIVE *nods. He kisses her hand. A little pause. They look at each other.* MAHOMET'S *head rises at back in the veranda over a shrub; he listens a moment or two and withdraws.*)

OLIVE. You remember what we arranged ?

CARNAC. Yes.

OLIVE. Say it over to me.

CARNAC. A tiger-lily, and I come to you. A rose, and you come to me here.

OLIVE. And the time?

CARNAC. The number of notches in the paper that binds the flower signifies the hour.

OLIVE. Faithful scholar ! Word perfect !

CARNAC. And when——?

OLIVE. I can't say exactly, because I shall have to contrive. But I shall send you a tiger-lily or a rose before this evening. (*He kisses her hand.*) If I come here how shall I get in ?

CARNAC (*pointing to door,* R.). Come to that door. Knock gently. I will let you in.

OLIVE. Hush ! Someone coming !

> (*Going to door,* L., *listening.*)

CARNAC (*quickly opens door*, R.). This way. Till this evening !

> (*Snatches a kiss from her hand as she goes off. As* CARNAC *gets her off*, MAHOMET *again looks in at window, and then withdraws.* CARNAC *closes door*, R. *Enter* SCRIVENER, *door* L., *shown in by* ALI KHAN. *Exit* ALI KHAN.)

SCRIVENER. Good-morning, Carnac.

CARNAC. Good-morning, sir.

SCRIVENER (*calls off at the door*, L.). Orderly !

Enter ALI BUSHA, *the* GENERAL'S *orderly*, L.

ORDERLY. Sahib ?   (*Salaams.*)

GENERAL. Go over to Mr. Barton and ask him to bring his Highness the Rajah to me here.

ORDERLY. Yes, Sahib.

> (*Salaams in going.*)

SCRIVENER. Was that Major Radnage whom I saw coming along the road ?

ORDERLY. Yes, Sahib.

SCRIVENER. Ask him to step in here.

ORDERLY. Yes, Sahib.

> (*Salaams and exit*, L.)

SCRIVENER (*tossing a note to* CARNAC, *who takes it and reads it*). I've just had that note from Hartford. He's holding the enquiry on Radnage this morning.   It was a mere chance that the hospital and every man in it weren't burned alive through Radnage's drunken carelessness.

CARNAC (*has read note and gives it back to* GENERAL.).   Poor Billy!   I suppose it wouldn't be possible to stretch a point again in his favour ?

SCRIVENER.   No, I've made up my mind. He goes this time!   Ah!   (*As* RADNAGE *enters*, L., *shown in by* ALI KHAN, *who goes off*.   RAD-NAGE *is very deeply ashamed, tries to hide it*.) Now, Major Radnage!

RADNAGE.   Sir !

SCRIVENER.   I sent for you to give you a friendly hint.   You'll be well advised to send in your papers at once.

RADNAGE.   I had been hard at work all the day, sir, without anything to eat, and I hadn't closed my eyes for two nights before.   Wouldn't it be possible, sir, for you and Major Hartford just to close your eyes to my folly for this once ?   Couldn't you take a little nap, General, and let my damned drunken tomfoolery pass by the while, and then wake up and forget all about it, or say to me, "Radnage, you tipsy rascal, you might have sacrificed a dozen brave men's lives, but the special Providence that watches over children and drunkards, and you, was on the look-out and kept them safe.   And

so for the sake of old times at Kandahar, I'll do
my best to get it passed over this once."
(*Pause. The* GENERAL *is silent.*) Did I hear
you say that, General? Thank you! Thank
you!

SCRIVENER.   No. I didn't say it. I've just
had a note from Major Hartford.

RADNAGE.   I knew Hartford would go
against me.

SCRIVENER.   Don't you deserve it?

RADNAGE.   I deserve to be hanged, whipped,
and kicked out of the service. But is there one
of us, sir, the best man living—you yourself,
General—would you dare to lift up your head
again if your Superior Officer (*with an inclina-
tion of the hand towards heaven*) were to show
you all your mistakes and follies chalked up
against you, and say, "That's your score, General Scrivener. Pay up."

SCRIVENER (*without taking his eyes from his
papers, in a dry, unmoved tone*). You'd better
send in your papers at once.

(RADNAGE *looks very downcast, and is
going off.* CARNAC *goes up to him.*)

CARNAC.   If I can do anything for you, Billy
—take a passage for you to England, or——

RADNAGE.   No, thank you, Carnac.

CARNAC.   What do you mean to do?

RADNAGE.   Oh, just hang about here, and

cadge on all you good fellows, and drink myself to death. The worst of it is I've got such a good constitution, and I'm so thoroughly seasoned, I'm afraid it will be a very long and tough job for me; but (*buttoning up his coat with resolution*) I daresay I shall be equal to it. (*To* SCRIVENER.) Good day, sir.

SCRIVENER. Good day, Major Radnage.

CARNAC. Come to me by-and-by and I'll see what I can do for you.

RADNAGE. Don't you be such an idiot as to waste another thought or another sixpence on me, Colonel. Good-by.

(*Exit*, L. CARNAC *looks after him.*)

CARNAC. Poor Billy! Here comes our prisoner!

SCRIVENER. Shall we be able to get anything out of the rascal?

CARNAC. We can but try——and be prepared for the worst.

Enter BEARER, *showing in the* RAJAH OF MOTIALA, BARTON, *and* GUARD.

SCRIVENER (*with profound bow*). Good-morning, your Highness. (RAJAH *salaams.*)

CARNAC. Good-morning, your Highness.

RAJAH (*salaams*). May I ask, Sahib, why my suite is not allowed to accompany me here?

SCRIVENER. We wish to speak privately with you, Prince.

RAJAH. I have no desire to speak privately with you, Sahib.

SCRIVENER. It is in your Highness's interest.

RAJAH. You will perhaps allow me to judge what is for my interest. Have I your permission to retire, Sahib?

SCRIVENER. No. Mr. Barton, take your men off and wait within call. (BARTON *takes off his men*, L., *leaving* GENERAL, CARNAC *and* RAJAH.) We know that your Highness is in communication with the Rajah of Sirhoot and the Nawab of Fyzapore.

(RAJAH *salaams unmoved.*)

CARNAC. We have stopped your spies, Maharajah, and I have your correspondence here.

(*Producing papers from desk and holding them to* RAJAH.)

RAJAH (*unmoved*). Then there is no necessity for me to ͵acquaint you with anything further, Sahib.

CARNAC. Yes. From what we have here we learn that you are inciting the Rajah of Sirhoot to rise, and you have arranged that he shall be joined at a concerted time and place by your scattered troops.

RAJAH (*same demeanour*). Indeed, Sahib.

SCRIVENER. It will be to your advantage, Prince, to give us the particulars of that place of meeting and the time—in the strictest confidence.

RAJAH. How will that be to my advantage, Sahib ?

SCRIVENER. If you communicate these particulars truthfully, I shall send you to Calcutta to be tried by the civil power with a recommendation that you shall be dealt with leniently.

RAJAH. And if I do not communicate those particulars ?

SCRIVENER. Then I shall try you this afternoon, Prince, and if you are found guilty I shall have your Highness shot to-morrow morning. (RAJAH *salaams and says nothing.*) Has your Highness anything to say ?

RAJAH. Nothing, Sahib.

SCRIVENER (*goes to door, calls*). Mr. Barton (*enter* BARTON), will you please take his Highness and bring him up for trial this afternoon at four, as arranged.

BARTON. Yes, sir. (*Signs at the door to his men. They enter.*) If your Highness is ready.

> (RAJAH *salaams profoundly to* SCRIVENER
> *and* CARNAC, *and exit, followed by*
> BARTON *and soldiers.* SCRIVENER *and*
> CARNAC *look at each other with a*
> *grin and a shrug.*)

SCRIVENER. Nothing to be got out of him.

(CARNAC *walks a step or two, then, as if struck with an idea.*)

CARNAC. Sir — If I may suggest — try him at the Ghŭr-i-nōor. March him and his suite publicly through the town first, and let it be known that any spy who is in his pay or confidence will be amply rewarded for bringing any information.

SCRIVENER. Good. Very good. Arrange that, will you?

CARNAC. I will, sir.

SCRIVENER. Good-morning.

CARNAC. Good-morning, sir. (*Exit* SCRIVENER. CARNAC *is following him. As* CARNAC *is going off* MAHOMET *appears on the veranda.* CARNAC *happens to turn back for a moment, sees* MAHOMET *there.*) What are you doing there?

MAHOMET. Syrett Sahib sends his salaam, and he will be glad to know whether his presence will be required at the council this morning?

CARNAC (*curtly*). If the General sends for him.

(*Exit*, L., MAHOMET *creeps after him.*)

SCENE II

THE GHŬR-I-NŎOR AND BAZAAR, DILGHAUT.
LARGE FULL SCENE.

*The Ghŭr-i-nŏor takes up the back of the stage; it is
a large building of Hindoo architecture, with a
large flight of steps. To the R. a bazaar, with
workers in it; to the L., archways of Hindoo
architecture, with images, etc. Time, the afternoon.*

*Discover passers-by, bheesties, etc., and on steps a
group of English officers,* BELL, LOVATT *and* HOBBS
—looking off L.

BELL.   What are you loafing about here for,
Padri ?

LOVATT.   Padri thinks if they sentence the
Rajah to be shot there will be a chance for him
to sneak in a little spiritual consolation, don't
you, Padri ?

HOBBS.   No, my boy.   I shall reserve my
exercise of that particular function till I'm
appointed chaplain of Newgate, and get a
chance of practising upon you some fine morning.   Rely upon me to improve the occasion
and give you a good send-off.

        (*Noise of an approaching crowd in the
        distance.   Enter* SCRIVENER *and*
        SYRETT, R.   *They go up a few steps
        and stand still, looking off in the di-
        rection of the approaching crowd.*)

SYRETT. Then you are going to try the
Rajah at the Ghŭ-i-nōor, sir.

SCRIVENER. Yes. I thought it would make
a good impression to lead him through the
town.

Enter CARNAC, *with native soldier dragging
on* CHRISTNA, *a native spy.*

CARNAC (*to* GENERAL). I have some most
important news, sir. I set a watch on the Rajah, and I discovered that he had sent this man
with this despatch to the Rajah of Sirhoot.
(*Giving the despatch to* SCRIVENER.) It seems
the whole province is ready to burst into a
blaze All the forces under the Rajah of Sirhoot are in mutiny, and meet to-night under his
command to march on Dilghaut. (SCRIVENER
glances through the despatch.) Bring that rascal
here ! We caught him red-handed ! (*Aside to*
SCRIVENER.) It's all right, sir. The blackguard
has sold me the despatches for ten rupees, but
I've got to pretend to take him prisoner to save
his skin from his comrades.

(*The* RAJAH *is led in, attended by his suite and
a guard of soldiers in charge of* BARTON,
a large crowd following, RADNAGE *amongst
them.* MAHOMET *creeps on and watches*
CARNAC *during the following scene. When
the crowd disperses* MAHOMET *creeps behind
a pillar where he can still watch* CARNAC.)

Rajah (*recognising the spy*). You've turned
traitor ?

Native. No, mighty Highness! I had
started on my journey to do the great commands of your mighty Highness, but the Sahib
Carnac rode after me and took me captive and
brought me back by the hair of my head,
accursed may he be for ever, and his children,
and his children's children.

Scrivener (*having read the despatch*). Your
Highness, I need not ask you again for any
details of the insurrection. I have them all
here under your Highness's seal. Mr. Barton,
take his Highness into the Ghŭr-i-nōor, and we
will try him by court-martial at once.

Rajah. Your time is very valuable, Sahib ;
I will not trouble you to waste any of it
upon me.

> (*He has a small bottle of poison in his hand ; he
> puts it suddenly to his lips and drains it off.
> The English officers rush to him and try to
> stop him. He puts them away and drops
> the poison bottle, smiling at them.*)

Scrivener. Major Radnage, will you please
look to his Highness?

> (Radnage *goes to the* Rajah.)

Rajah. It is too late, Sahib. You will also
find it too late to stop the insurrection. My
ally, the Maharajah of Sirhoot, has taken all his

measures. Fyzapore will be in our hands to-morrow night. Dilghaut will be in our hands in one week. Barton Sahib, I am at your service for the remainder of my life.

SCRIVENER. Take him away, Mr. Barton. Major Radnage, see if anything can be done !

> (*They advance to take him, but he waves them away, and makes a profound salaam with his left hand.* BARTON, LOVATT, *and officers hurry him off. Exeunt* BARTON, LOVATT, BELL, HOBBS, *and* RADNAGE, *with* RAJAH *and suite, followed by the crowd.* MAHOMET *stays and stealthily watches* CARNAC *from a point of view open to the audience, but concealed from* CARNAC. CARNAC, SCRIVENER, *and* SYRETT *remain on the steps,* SCRIVENER *anxiously mastering the contents of the despatch.*)

SCRIVENER. This is serious, Carnac. We must call out every man at once, and march early to-morrow.

CARNAC. What about Fyzapore, sir ?

SCRIVENER. The palace is defensible. Don't you think they can hold out ?

CARNAC. How long, sir ?

SCRIVENER. If this information is correct I shall want every man that I have, and with the best of luck it will take me a week at least — a fortnight, perhaps, to stamp it out. They can hold out that time?

CARNAC. If they had a man to orga: ze the defence. But they've got nobody there that's worth his salt.

SCRIVENER. You must go, Carnac.

CARNAC (*taken aback*). I'd rather go to the front with you, sir, and get some fighting. There's nothing to be done at Fyzapore. If I may suggest —— Colonel Syrett ——

SYRETT. Thank you, Colonel Carnac. (*To* GENERAL.) I'm not acquainted with Fyzapore, sir. Colonel Carnac knows every inch of it.

> (*The* GENERAL *looks at both men in indecision, walks a step or two, they both appeal to him mutely, and wait for his decision with anxious expectation.*)

SCRIVENER (*at length*). You see from this (*indicating despatch*), the Nawab is lying low somewhere, and he'll try to rally his men the moment he knows I've marched from Dilghaut. You must go to Fyzapore, Carnac.

> (CARNAC'S *countenance falls with intense disappointment.*)

CARNAC. Very well, sir! (*Mutters.*) My rotten luck again!

Enter RADNAGE.

SCRIVENER. What about the Rajah, Major Radnage?

RADNAGE. Gone, sir. Went off with the usual beatific serenity of an aged sinner.

CARNAC. I shall be rather short of men, sir, at Fyzapore. Will you allow me to take Major Radnage with me?

SCRIVENER (*after a moment*). Very well.

CARNAC. I'm going to Fyzapore, Billy, to tinker up the palace defences, bully the natives, and keep our women from hysterics. Will you come with me?

RADNAGE. Delighted, Colonel! And, whether it's killing men or curing ladies, you shall find me equal to it, and you shall never regret giving me another chance.

(*Warmly shaking hands with* CARNAC.)

CARNAC. Bring plenty of bromide, Billy. It's the only weapon we shall want at Fyzapore.

Enter OLIVE *furtively, seen only at first by* CARNAC. *She has a letter in her hand which she shows to him secretly.*

SCRIVENER. Colonel Syrett, will you be at my bungalow in a quarter of an hour to consult about our march to-morrow morning?

SYRETT. Yes, sir.

SCRIVENER. Carnac. You will start for Fyzapore of course to-night.

CARNAC (*looking at* OLIVE). To-night, sir?

SCRIVENER. As soon as possible. When can you be ready?

CARNAC. At eight — (OLIVE *slightly frowns and shakes her head*) or ten. Rely on me, sir, that I'll be in the palace by to-morrow morning.

SCRIVENER. Very well. (*He is going off, sees* OLIVE, *stops a moment.*) Colonel Carnac, you will start at the earliest possible moment.

CARNAC. Yes, sir.

> (SCRIVENER *bows to* OLIVE *and exit.*
> OLIVE *comes up to* CARNAC *and* SYRETT.)

OLIVE. Where are you going to-night, Colonel Carnac?

CARNAC. To Fyzapore.

OLIVE. At what time?

CARNAC. At the earliest possible moment.

OLIVE. Will it be dangerous?

CARNAC. About as dangerous as a Hyde Park review.

OLIVE (*comes up between them, turns very sweetly to* SYRETT, *and behind her back gives* CARNAC *the letter as she is speaking to* SYRETT.

CARNAC *takes letter, shows great delight. To*
SYRETT). Are you going to Fyzapore, too,
Colonel Syrett?

SYRETT. No. I march with the General
to-morrow morning to stop the Rajah of
Sirhoot.

OLIVE. Will that be dangerous?

SYRETT. We shall have some fighting.

OLIVE. I wish you every success.

SYRETT. Thank you.

OLIVE (*she is going off,* SYRETT *is following
her*). No, please don't come. (*To* CARNAC.)
I wish you every success to-night, Colonel
Carnac.

CARNAC. Thank you. (*Exit* OLIVE.) Arthur,
you are the lucky man again.

> (*Exit, holding the letter in front of him so
> that* SYRETT *cannot see it.* SYRETT *is
> going off when* MAHOMET *creeps out to
> him.*)

MAHOMET (*salaams*). Sahib, the thief will
steal the Memsahib's jewels to-night.

SYRETT. I'll have nothing to do with it.
(*Pause.*) You won't wait till he has stolen the
jewels before you ——

MAHOMET. Do not fear, Sahib. He shall
not steal the jewels. Why do you look at me
like that, Sahib? Carnac Sahib will never go
to Fyzapore. There will be an accident. Or

perhaps it will not be an accident. Perhaps Carnac Sahib will know it is Mahomet Ali who strikes him before he can steal the Memsahib's jewels, and then all men shall know that Mahomet Ali will not suffer to be struck by Carnac Sahib. Mahomet Ali will strike back, and then a good stout English rope will go queek round my throat. Queek !

SYRETT. I'll have nothing to do with it.

> (*Exit.* MAHOMET *is going off, meets* SEETA, *who enters from behind a pillar.*)

MAHOMET. Ah, my sister ! Attend to me. I will not be followed.

SEETA. My brother, tell me you will do no evil to Carnac Sahib.

MAHOMET. Evil to Carnac Sahib ! Let me die the death of the wicked if I harm a hair of his head. The noble Carnac Sahib ! Why should I harm him ? (*Is going off, she is following him, he turns round savagely.*) Follow me not, Seeta. If thou dost, I will kill thee.

> (*Waves her off. Exit.* SEETA *stands looking after him as the stage grows dark, creeps after him.*)

(*Scene closed in by Scene III.*)

Scene III

Room in Carnac's Bungalow — Night — Half-past Seven

Discover Carnac *with a letter, notched on the fly-leaf, and a rose.*

Carnac (*reads the letter*). "Faithful scholar, I bring you a rose! Read truly its deep meaning, and count how many notches there are in this paper!" (*Counts*) One, two, three, four, five, six, seven, eight — (*reading*). Was ever such rotten luck! To be sent to that hole to-night! To be dished out of all the fighting and nearly all the love-making! (*Looking at watch.*) Quarter past seven! She'll be here at eight! I must start at ten! (*Skips over a couch on his way to door,* L., *as* Mahomet's *face peeps from behind the curtains, and then withdraws. Calls off,* L.) Syce!

    (Carnac *comes center, pressing the rose to his lips.*)

Syce (*enters and salaams*). Sahib!

Carnac. Have Bay Margaret saddled for me at ten. Give her a big feed and rub her down well, for I shall ride her like the devil. Have Emperor saddled for yourself, and Mischief for the other Syce. We start for Fyzapore at ten to the minute!

H

Syce.   At ten to the minute, Sahib.
                              (*Salaams and exit.*)
Carnac (*returns, takes the rose*).   And now
to kick my heels for half an hour——

Enter Ali Khan, l.

Ali.   A lady to see you, Sahib.
Carnac (*with great surprise and delight*).
Show her in.   (*Exit* Ali Khan.)   Good luck!
Good luck!   (Ali Khan *shows in* Ellice.)
Carnac (*surprised*).   Miss Ford!
Ellice.   I must speak to you alone.   (*To*
Ali Khan.)   Ask my Ayah to wait outside for
me.   (*Exit* Ali Khan.)
Carnac.   I'm afraid I can only give you a
few minutes——
Ellice (*much agitated*).   Forgive my com-
ing to you like this.   You are in great danger.
Carnac.   Danger?
Ellice.   You will be killed to-night if
you——
Carnac.   If I?
Ellice.   You mustn't go anywhere to-
night.
Carnac.   I must go to Fyzapore by-and-by.
Ellice.   You mustn't go alone; and till
you start you mustn't be alone for a moment.
Carnac.   I don't understand you.

ELLICE. Promise me you won't see — any-one — till you start for Fyzapore.

CARNAC. A moment ago you said I was not to be alone for a moment. Now you say I must not see anyone.

ELLICE. You must not see one particular person. If you do you will be killed.

CARNAC. What particular person must I not see to-night?

ELLICE (*embarrassed*). Don't you know?

(CARNAC *turns away, abashed, takes a turn or two as if in deep thought.*)

CARNAC. Thank you very much. I am warned, and I will guard against any possible danger.

ELLICE. You can't. It will come when you least expect it.

CARNAC. I will take all precautions. Now you must let me say good-night——

(*Taking out watch.*)

ELLICE. Ah! Don't look at your watch. You must not go — you shall not. I did not mean to speak like that, but if you don't be-lieve me, I don't know what I shall do. You won't go?

CARNAC. Tell me all you know. Speak quite plainly.

ELLICE. My Ayah is the sister of Maho-met Ali, Colonel Syrett's bearer, and she is

to be married to Mrs. Arnison's bearer.
(MAHOMET ALI *creeps out at back from cur-*
tain with a lifted knife.) She is very faithful
to me. To-night she has learned from Mrs.
Arnison's bearer that —— Ask Colonel Syrett
—— he knows —— !

 CARNAC. Colonel Syrett knows what?

> (ELLICE *suddenly sees* MAHOMET ALI, *who is*
> *rushing at him with the lifted knife. She*
> *screams, and* CARNAC *turns round just in*
> *time to catch* MAHOMET'S *hand, seizes* MA-
> HOMET, *takes the knife from him, and*
> *throws him on the ground.*)

 ELLICE (*goes to door. Calls*). Bearer!
Bearer! Syce! Quick!

 CARNAC (*to* ELLICE). You were right! I
was in danger.

Enter ALI KHAN *and two or three servants,* L.

 CARNAC. Take this man and put him under arrest. Go to Colonel Syrett and ask him
to please come here to me at once. Take
care that man does not escape.

 ALI. He shall not escape, Sahib.

> (MAHOMET *is taken off,* L., *by* ALI KHAN
> *and servants.*)

 ELLICE (*who is frightened and half crying*).
You are not hurt?

CARNAC. Not a scratch. I should have been killed if it hadn't been for you. Thank you with all my heart. Am I in any further danger?

ELLICE. I don't know. Seeta got it all from Mrs. Arnison's bearer. He says that Colonel Syrett knew you were to be killed to-night.

CARNAC. Impossible. Impossible!

ELLICE. At least — promise me now ——

CARNAC. What?

ELLICE. There may be others watching for you. Promise me you won't go where — where your life may be in danger.

CARNAC. How can I tell where my life may be in danger?

> (*Going to table, his eye falls on the letter and rose — she sees them too — an embarrassed pause.*)

ELLICE (*is going off at door; she turns with great reproach*). You might at least promise me you will run no further risk to-night.

CARNAC. Miss Ford, I promise you that I will run no risk to-night, except such as you would wish a good soldier to run.

ELLICE. Thank you! Thank you! (*Embarrassed.*) My Ayah is waiting for me. I must go ——

Enter ALI KHAN, *announces* SYRETT SAHIB.
Enter SYRETT, *exit* ALI KHAN.   SYRETT
bows to ELLICE.

SYRETT.   You sent for me?

CARNAC.   I have your bearer under arrest.

SYRETT.   What for?

CARNAC.   He has tried to stab me.   Have
you anything to say?

(*Watching him keenly.*)

SYRETT (*after a pause*).   No.

CARNAC.   Do you know what the rascal's
accomplice says?——

SYRETT (*alarmed*).   What?

CARNAC (*to* ELLICE).   I wish to give Colonel
Syrett the opportunity of denying what I am
sure is an unjust charge.

ELLICE.   Mrs. Arnison's bearer told my
Ayah that you knew that your bearer meant
to kill Colonel Carnac to-night.

CARNAC.   It's false?

SYRETT.   Of course it's false!   Of course
it's false!   Have you anything more to say
to me?   (*Going.*)

CARNAC.   Yes.   Please wait a moment.
Miss Ford, I am glad that you have heard
Colonel Syrett's denial.   Will you leave me
a moment with Colonel Syrett?

ELLICE.   Good-night.

CARNAC. No, not good-night. I want to
see you before I start for Fyzapore. (*Exit*
ELLICE. *He closes the door carefully after her.*
Watching SYRETT *keenly.*) So you knew nothing of this business?

SYRETT. Don't I tell you I knew nothing?

CARNAC. Give me your word of honour you
knew nothing of it.

SYRETT. Don't I tell you I knew nothing!
(*Is going.*)

CARNAC (*stopping him*). Your word of
honour as an English officer and a gentleman
—you knew nothing of it?
(*A very long pause.*)

SYRETT (*at length*). I did know of it, damn
you!

CARNAC. Ah! ah! and you promised to
fight fair!

SYRETT. Fight me now!

CARNAC. Fight you! Fight a man who
sets an assassin to stab me in the back!

SYRETT. I didn't set him on! You kicked
the man and he threatened to kill you. It
was his quarrel, not mine.

CARNAC. But you knew of it!

SYRETT. It was no affair of mine. Fight
me! Fight me!

CARNAC. I'll see you damned before I'll
fight you!

SYRETT. Fight me! Fight me!

CARNAC. Not I! My life's worth too much just now to throw it away on you, even if it was allowed in the service. And you promised to fight fair!

SYRETT. I will fight fair! Fight me! Fight me, or——

(*Raises his hand to strike* CARNAC.)

CARNAC. Look here you fool, if you strike me I shall have to get you court-martialled, and all this dirty business will leak out. Give me a chance of hushing it up for the sake of the old times. I don't want to spoil your future career. Say that you're sorry! Say that you were led away by anger, madness, jealousy; say anything that will let me see a bit of the gentleman and man of honour left in you! Come now, old fellow, don't force me to get you kicked out of the service.

SYRETT (*after a little pause*). I'm sorry. I have behaved like a skunk and a blackguard. But I was mad with jealousy. I'm ashamed of myself.

CARNAC. Say no more.

SYRETT. I'm ready to go to the General and tell him all if you wish.

CARNAC. What good would that do? Take the rascal away with you. Give him as much money as will shut his mouth, and

kick him to the other end of India. Then
forget what has happened to-night. I'll forget it too.

SYRETT.   I'll never forget what you've
done for me to-night, Carnac. My life is at
your service if you need it.

CARNAC.   I don't at present, thank you,
only don't keep on threatening to take mine,
there's a good fellow.

SYRETT.   You won't shake hands with me,
I suppose?

CARNAC.   I'd rather not just now, if you
don't mind. But I will when you've done
something to wash this out.

SYRETT.   Good-night.

CARNAC.   Good-night.

> (*Exit* SYRETT. *Left alone,* CARNAC *goes to
> the table, takes up the letter and the rose,
> shows a struggle, burns the letter in the
> lamp, goes to veranda, throws the rose
> away, comes down. A knock at door,* L.
> *Pause. Another knock. He goes towards
> door.* OLIVE'S *voice heard on other side
> of door.*)

OLIVE.   Are you alone?

Enter ALI KHAN, L.

ALI.   Mr. Barton.   (*Exit.*)

Enter BARTON *in great excitement, salutes.*

BARTON.   The Nawab has surrounded Fyzapore, sir, and has taken several of our native
soldiers and put their eyes out.   He is threatening the Palace, but we're holding it.   The
General says it's a desperate job, and he can
only spare you Kynaston's Company.   Will
you take them on to Fyzapore, throw them
into the Palace, and hold it if possible?

CARNAC.   Right.   I'll start this moment.
By Jove, I've got the fighting after all!

BARTON.   I congratulate you, sir.   The
General says the native soldiers will want
some British stiffening, and you may take
one or two volunteers, sir.

ALI KHAN (*re-entering*).   Captain Bell and
Mr. Lovatt wish to speak to you at once,
Sahib, on important business.

CARNAC.   Show them in.

(*Exit* ALI KHAN.)

BARTON.   They want you to take them, sir.
I hope you won't leave me out in the cold,
sir.

Re-enter ALI KHAN, *showing in* BELL *and*
LOVATT.   *Exit* ALI KHAN.

BELL.   I beg pardon, sir.   I wish to volunteer to go with you in the forlorn hope to-night to Fyzapore.

LOVATT. I hope you'll take me, sir. You know you can rely upon me, sir.

CARNAC. How many did the General say I can take?

BARTON. The General said "One or two," sir. I hope you won't forget what I did at Blakepore, sir.

LOVATT. You had that chance, Barton. I hope you'll consider it's my turn now, sir.

(*They all stand in mute supplication.*)

CARNAC. Captain Bell and Mr. Barton, I'll take you with me.

(LOVATT *bursts into tears.*)

BELL. Thank you, sir, thank you! I'm much obliged to you, sir!

BARTON. Thank you! Thank you, sir!

CARNAC. Captain Bell, parade the Company and bring them here at once.

BELL. Yes, sir.   (*Exit.*)

CARNAC. Mr. Barton, see that a day's provisions are prepared, and the horses brought round at once.

BARTON. Yes, sir.   (*Exit.*)

CARNAC. Come, Mr. Lovatt——

LOVATT. Do take me, sir! You shall never regret it! I'll fight like old Nick for you, sir! Do take me!

CARNAC. The General said one or two. I've chosen two.

LOVATT. I think I can get the General's permission, sir. Do take me, sir!

CARNAC. Very well. If the General can spare you.

LOVATT. Thank you, sir.

Enter ALI KHAN, *showing in* HOBBS.
Exit LOVATT.

CARNAC. What now, Padri?

HOBBS. I beg pardon, Colonel. I've just heard you've got a good thing on at Fyzapore, and want a few handy chaps. I hope you'll let me ride with you.

CARNAC. I'm already full, Padri. And there'll be more fighting than praying, I expect.

HOBBS. Well, sir, I know I'm an awful duffer at my own profession, but I think I should be a bit of a flyer at the other. Barton and Lovatt have done nothing but chaff me about my cloth ever since I've been here, and I want to show them that when it comes to being cut to bits, I'm just as good a man as they are, and perhaps better.

CARNAC. All right, Padri. If you get the General's consent.

HOBBS.   Thank you, sir.   I'm awfully obliged.   I'll get my pony round, and (*very much excited*) God bless you, sir!   I'll get my pony round!   God bless you!   God bless you!

CARNAC (*goes to door* R.).   Mrs. Arnison! (OLIVE *enters.*)   You heard?

OLIVE.   Yes.

CARNAC.   I've not a moment to spare. Good-bye.

OLIVE.   You sha'n't go.   I won't let you.

CARNAC.   What!

OLIVE   You can be ill—or—find some other excuse.   When you get a little way out, send them on and ride back to me.

CARNAC.   What!

OLIVE.   Ride back to me.   I'll meet you. You can still get to Fyzapore in the morning.

CARNAC.   Meantime all the English may be murdered.

OLIVE.   Then you'll be too late to rescue them, and you'll only be killed yourself.

CARNAC.   That's no reason for sneaking out of it.   Now will you please excuse me?

OLIVE.   Colonel Carnac, if you don't ride back to me to-night there's an end to everything between us.

CARNAC.   All right.   Good-bye.

OLIVE   I hate you!   I hate you!

(SCRIVENER'S *voice heard off* L.)

SCRIVENER.   Say I must see him at once.

CARNAC.   The General! (*Points to door* R. *She makes as if to stay.*)   For God's sake!   Do you wish to ruin yourself?

> (*She goes off,* R., *but not before* SCRIVENER *enters* L., *shown in by* ALI KHAN, *in time to see her as she goes off. Exit* OLIVE, R. *Exit* ALI KHAN.)

SCRIVENER (*very sternly*).   Colonel Carnac, I sent you an order to start for Fyzapore, and I find you——

CARNAC.   You find me ready, sir.   Your order came three minutes ago.   (*Goes up, looks out from veranda.*)   My horse is saddled, and the men are now on parade.

Enter, L., ELLICE.

ELLICE.   Sir Hardinge — Colonel Carnac! You've heard?

CARNAC.   What?

ELLICE.   The Nawab is in Fyzapore.   He's putting out their eyes.   My father!   My sister! I must go to them.   You'll take me?

CARNAC.   My dear Miss Ford, it's impossible.

ELLICE.   If you don't take me I shall come on by myself.

CARNAC.   You will never be so foolish.

ELLICE.   Whatever happens, I shall come on myself.   Sir Hardinge, you'll let me go?

SCRIVENER. My dear young lady, you are mad to dream of it. Carnac, the men are on parade outside.   (*Exit at veranda.*)

CARNAC. Yes, sir.

ELLICE (*to* CARNAC). I must go to them. Take me to-night.

CARNAC. Impossible. But if I get there to-night without being cut to bits, and it's possible to get you into the Palace, I will send an escort for you to-morrow night.

ELLICE. You won't fail me?

CARNAC. I won't fail you. Good-bye.

ELLICE. Good-bye.

CARNAC. If I come out of this——

SCRIVENER (*voice heard off*). Colonel Carnac!

Enter BARTON, LOVATT, HOBBS, BELL, *and* RADNAGE.

CARNAC. Now my lads. Steady march to Fyzapore. We shall reach there at four to-morrow morning, and at five we must either be inside the Palace or every man of us must be chopped to pieces outside it.

> (*Exeunt all except* ELLICE. *Word of command given. Military music.* ELLICE *watching.*)

Seventeen days elapse between Acts III and IV.

ACT IV

Scene I

THE JEWELLED PALACE AT FYZAPORE, a magnificent
building of Mohammedan architecture, with arches
at back, showing the outer wall, which overlooks a
stretch of Indian plain.

Entrances R. *and* L., *and at back. The walls are
broken and cracked in places, giving indications of
a siege. Time, sunset. A large table is set at back
with tinned meats, biscuits, champagne, coffee, etc.*

Discover ELLICE *busy making coffee at the table, and
arranging the table for a meal, helped by* AMINA.
MRS. WHITMORE, *a very pale, delicate lady, about
thirty, is seated at back on the steps. Her face is
rigid with despair ; her eyes staring. She looks
steadfastly in front of her, sometimes wringing
her hands, but otherwise taking no notice. All the
faces of the besieged throughout this scene are very
pale and drawn with fright and despair. In the
middle of the stage* CARNAC *is sleeping in the
sprawling attitude of one overcome with fatigue.*
MAY FORD, *an English girl of eleven, is bending
over him, fanning him to keep the flies away.*
ELLICE *goes to* MRS. WHITMORE.

(112)

ELLICE. Come! Try and eat something.

MRS. WHITMORE. Let me be. Let me be! Why doesn't Colonel Carnac surrender and let them come and murder us? Then we should be at peace.

(ELLICE, *with a gesture of helplessness, comes to* MAY.)

MAY. She hasn't any pluck, has she?

ELLICE. Hush, dear. Her mind is going, poor creature.

FORD (*entering very hurriedly*). Where's the Colonel?

ELLICE (*pointing to* CARNAC). He said he might have a heavy night's work, and he must get a snatch of sleep to be ready for it. He began to eat, but he dropped down dead asleep before he had taken a mouthful. Don't wake him. Think how long he has been on the watch.

FORD. Poor fellow. He's right. I ought not to disturb him.

ELLICE. Is anything the matter?

FORD. Those blackguard native soldiers are getting out of hand. They want to send a message to the Nawab and give up the Palace.

ELLICE. He knows that. He has disarmed them. Don't wake him.

FORD. My poor girl, you are fagged to death, too. What possessed you to come here

I

when you were safe at Dilghaut? What possessed Carnac to send for you?

ELLICE.   He promised me faithfully that if
it was possible to get me into the Palace he
would send for me, and he kept his word.
Do you think I could have stayed there when
I thought they were putting your eyes out?

MAY.   The Nawab daren't put my eyes out.
I had a sword, and I should have simply cleft
him where he stood.

FORD (*smiles at* MAY, *turns to* ELLICE).   Give
me a mouthful of something, dear. I'll take
it with me and go back and help Bell and
Lovatt to keep those scoundrels down. What
is there?   (*Going to table.*)

ELLICE (*following him*).   Only the tinned
things and biscuit. All the wine has gone,
except champagne. They've found another
dozen cases in the stores, so there's plenty of
that. And tea and coffee.

FORD.   I'll take enough for Lovatt and
Bell, and myself. We sha'n't be able to
leave those blackguards for a moment.

                (*Taking things from the table.*)

MRS. WHITMORE (*rises, wringing her hands*).
Why doesn't Colonel Carnac give us up and
end it? Oh God, let them come in and kill
us and end it! End it, I say! End it! End
it!   (*Exit wringing her hands.*)

FORD. Poor creature. Still the same.

ELLICE. Just the same. I can't rouse her.

FORD. It won't be much longer for her. It won't be much longer for any of us.

MAY. Padri says that when all the powder is gone——

FORD (*alarmed, glancing round*). Hush, my darling! We mustn't let the soldiers know there's no powder.

MAY. Of course not. Still, Padri says that when all the powder is gone we must simply cut our way through, that's all. So you needn't get in a funk, daddy.

FORD. I won't get in a funk, dear. (*Calls* ELLICE *aside.*) I think to-night will end it, dear. If it should?

ELLICE. I think I shall be ready. I think my courage will hold out.

FORD. God bless you, dear. (*Kisses her. Points to* CARNAC.) If he wakes, tell him we are at the Guard-room doing our best to keep those devils down.

> (*Exit, taking champagne, tinned meat and biscuits.*)

ELLICE. Ayah, go to the hospital and tell Miss Lovelace and Major Radnage that you'll stay there whilst they come to dinner. (*Exit* AMINA.) May, go down the two mining shafts and tell Mr. Barton and Padri that the dinner is ready if they can be spared. I'll watch him.

> (*Pointing to* CARNAC. MAY *gives the fan
> to* ELLICE *and exit.* ELLICE *fans*
> CARNAC.)

Enter MADGE LOVELACE, *a haggard English
lady, about thirty. She comes up to* ELLICE
and kisses her.

ELLICE.   How is it in the hospital, dear?

MADGE.   Horrible! Horrible! Oh, the smell!   (*Shudders.*)

ELLICE.   How is everybody doing?

MADGE.   Miss Price and Miss Newson about the same. Poor Mrs. Pennithorne's much worse. I shall be down to-morrow. Don't I look ghastly?

ELLICE.   None of us look very beautiful.

MADGE.   You look interesting, at any rate, and I know I'm a hideous wreck. Ellice, ducky, I've lost my powder puff and box. What can I do?

ELLICE (*fanning* CARNAC).   I should do without it.

MADGE.   Lend me yours, ducky.

ELLICE.   I haven't got one.

MADGE.   How tiresome! Then I can't come to dinner.

ELLICE. Why not?

MADGE. Let the men see me like this!

ELLICE. I don't think they'll mind. We may all look very much worse to-morrow.

MADGE. Oh, don't give me the horrors. (*Looking down at* CARNAC.) How ill he looks!

ELLICE. This is the first sleep he's had for a week.

MADGE. I'd like to kiss him for all he's done for us.

ELLICE. He has been brave, hasn't he?

MADGE. Oh, if I do get out of this won't I let everybody in England know what plucky fellows we had with us. (*Blows a kiss to* CARNAC.) I must go and scrub myself down. Send me some dinner, will you? You are a donkey not to carry a powder puff with you.

   (*Exit. As* MADGE *goes off, noise of a shell exploding in the distance.* CARNAC *stirs and mutters in his sleep.*)

CARNAC. Look at that devil creeping under the wall there! Down with him! Bravo, Padri, bravo! If it weren't for the women, Billy, if it weren't for the women!

ELLICE. Ah!

CARNAC. If I fall tell Miss Ford ——(*Pause. Then solemnly, in the same voice as* KYNASTON'S.) Give up that woman or be lost for ever! All

right, Hedley, old fellow. (*Pause.*)   ELLICE!
ELLICE! (ELLICE *rises, startled and delighted.*)
Do you mind?   Take my hand.   He wishes it.
I wish it.

ELLICE.   Ah!

CARNAC (*half wakes, sits up, drops down
again with great fatigue; again stirs, tries to
rouse himself, looks at her, shakes himself*).
Where was I? (*Stretches himself.*)   Excuse me.
I'm — oh! —(*Shakes himself, tries to pull himself
together.*)   For heaven's sake don't let me go to
sleep.   (*Trying to rouse himself.*)

ELLICE.   I've got some fresh coffee.
                          (*Going to table.*)

CARNAC.   Thanks!   Thanks!   Don't let me
go to sleep. (ELLICE *goes with coffee.   Shakes
him a little.   Trying to rouse himself.*)   Eh?

ELLICE.   Some coffee!

CARNAC (*again shakes himself*).   Thanks.
(*Drinks coffee.*)   That's good.   If ever there
was a ministering angel, you've been one to
me this last fortnight.

Enter RADNAGE.

CARNAC.   How goes it, Billy?

RADNAGE.   Awful.   I felt I must get out of
it for a few minutes.   (*Going up to table.*)

Re-enter AMINA.

AMINA (*to* ELLICE).   If you please, Missie Memsahib, the old Memsahib Pennithorne will not let me nurse her.   She will call out for you.

ELLICE.   I'll go to her.

CARNAC.   Must you go ?

ELLICE.   It's only for a few minutes, and the poor old creature likes me to be near her.

> (*He looks very anxiously at her, kisses her hand, and then lets her go.   Exit* ELLICE, *followed by* AMINA.)

RADNAGE (*going up to the table*).   Ah ! Champagne.   Good.

CARNAC (*comes up to him, touches him on the shoulder*).   Billy !   Take care.

RADNAGE.   No fear, old fellow.   Whilst this excitement lasts I shall take my whack like a man, and I shall do my duty to my patients. But — but ——

CARNAC.   But what, Billy ?

RADNAGE.   The moment this danger is over I shall go flop, like a child's penny air balloon.

CARNAC.   No, Billy.

RADNAGE (*breaking down, half crying*).   Yes ! Yes !   If it were not for what I can still do for all you brave fellows and the women, I wish I could make a good end of it to-night, for I feel, I *know*, Carnac, that the moment I get out of this — if I do get out of it — this devil that I've kept behind me for the last fortnight will jump on my back and whip and spur me headlong to bottomless perdition.

CARNAC.   No, Billy, no.

RADNAGE.   I know it. But till then you needn't fear that I shall take one drop more than will make me physician extraordinary to those poor creatures in hospital and a jolly good companion to the dear brave fellows (*enter* HOBBS *and* BARTON, *in a hurry, followed by* MAY. *They come up to him, and he embraces* HOBBS *and* BARTON) and the dauntless young English Joan of Arc (*bowing to* MAY), who are now about to sit down to what may, or may not, be their last meal, and therefore, in either alternative, are going to do justice to it. Foregather ! Foregather ! (*They sit down.*) Menu ! Tinned herrings, biscuits, champagne ! (*The Indian tom-tom begins sounding outside.*) Band ! (*Shell explodes with a terrific noise.*) And fireworks !

BARTON (*holding up champagne as if he were reciting a grace*). Bless and praise the Nawab of Fyzapore for laying in a good stock of champagne for us to drink. Wish his taste had been for something a trifle drier.

RADNAGE.   My son Richard, to-morrow at this hour we may not only be without champagne, but without throats wherein to pour it. Therefore, fall to, and revile not.

CARNAC. Nothing fresh, Padri?

HOBBS. No, sir. Dicky and I have been down the shafts all the afternoon with our ears glued, but we can't hear anything.

BARTON. Pardon me, sir, our rascals won't work a counter mine, and we've got no powder left; so if the Nawab is mining us, don't you think we had better be comfortably blown up before we know anything about it?

CARNAC. There's something to be said for that, Dicky. (*With great concern.*) If we could but know what's going on outside! Why on earth don't we hear from the General? Ah, my lads, I thought I was clever to sneak you in here without losing a life; but I've only brought you into a death-trap!

(*Noise of men in mutiny without. They all rise.*)

CARNAC. What's that? (FORD *rushes in excitedly.*) What is it, Ford?

FORD. They've broken out, sir. We can't hold them in any longer. They demand the gates shall be opened to the Nawab.

LOVATT (*rushing in*). It's all over, sir, I'm afraid. Captain Bell is holding the gate. Can we save the ladies?

CARNAC (*takes a disturbed turn or two. To*
BARTON). There's no powder, Dicky?

BARTON. Not a cartridge.

CARNAC. Do as I tell you. One false
step and we're done for. Shush! (*Crowd of*
MUTINEERS *rush in headed by a* RINGLEADER.
CARNAC *stands very firm. The* RINGLEADER
comes up to CARNAC *and salaams.*) Well?

RINGLEADER. Pardon, Sahib. His Mighty
Highness the Nawab has offered us our lives
if the Palace is given up to-night.

CARNAC. Well?

RINGLEADER. We demand, Sahib, that you
shall open the gates to us and let us go out
to the Nawab. What is your answer, Sahib?

>(CARNAC *takes out his revolver, shoots the
> man. The man falls. The other* MUTI-
> NEERS *stand back a pace,* CARNAC *cover-
> ing them with his revolver.*)

CARNAC (*takes out a large key, gives it to*
BARTON). Mr. Barton, go down to the powder room, light a fuse, and the moment I
send the order, blow it up.

BARTON. Yes, sir.   (*Exit* BARTON.)

CARNAC. Mr. Hobbs, stand ready to take
the order.

HOBBS. Yes, sir.

CARNAC (*covering* MUTINEERS *with his revol-
ver*). If one of you takes a step further, or
tries to open the gates, I'll blow the Palace,

and us, and everyone of your damned car-
cases to rags and ribbons and eternity.
(*Murmurs of expostulation. The men begin to
fall back.*) But if you trust me and keep
quiet till General Scrivener comes to relieve
us, I promise that everyone of you shall have
fifty rupees and a medal, like the good brave
fellows that you are. Mr. Hobbs, stand
ready. Now, which shall it be? (*They all
murmur obedience and salaam. Murmurs :* "We
will obey you, Carnac Sahib. We will obey
you.") That's right. Mr. Lovatt, look after
these brave fellows. See that they are well
cared for. Let them have extra rations for
their fidelity, and (*aside in his ears*) for Heaven's
sake take care the blackguards don't get their
arms again. To your quarters at once. (*They
all go off murmuring,* "The noble Carnac Sahib."
Exit LOVATT.) Mr. Hobbs, tell Mr. Barton
to lock up the powder room and bring me
the key. (*Exit* HOBBS. *The wounded* MUTI-
NEER *stirs and groans. Calls off.*) Hi there!
Winged him! He'll get over it. (*Some* SOL-
DIERS *enter.*) Take him away and let him be
looked after! (*They remove the man.*) Now
we'll go on with our dinner. Let's have one
good meal before the end! (*They sit down.*)

(*Scene closed in by Scene II.*)

SCENE II

ROOM IN OLIVE ARNISON'S BUNGALOW

Door R. *Door at back,* L. *A looking glass. Discover*
OLIVE ARNISON in afternoon dress pacing up and
down in great impatience.

BEARER. The Sahib sends me to say that
he must start for Simla in two minutes.

OLIVE. Very well. (*The* BEARER *waits.*)
Very well. (*Exit* BEARER, *as* AYAH *enters at*
the outer door.)

OLIVE. Well? Did you see Colonel Syrett?
Did you give him my message?

AYAH. Yes, Memsahib. Colonel Syrett say
he is in a very great hurry, but he will come
to the Memsahib.

OLIVE. Wait for him at the side door.
Show him to me here. And then bring my
travelling things.

Enter MRS. REMINGTON *in outdoor dress, as*
if attired for a journey.

AYAH. Yes, Memsahib. (*Exit.*)

MRS. R. (*very sugary*). Olive, dearest, everything is ready. Charles is getting impatient.

OLIVE. Yes, I heard him swearing at the
Syce.

Mrs. R.   He says he must start at once.

Olive.   I won't keep him.

Mrs. R.   But, Olive, dearest, you are coming to Simla with us?

Olive.   Am I?

Mrs. R.   But we must be going.

Olive.   Must you?   Good-bye.

Mrs. R.   Olive dear, Charles says that as your husband he will insist upon your coming.

Olive.   Oh?   Ah!   Hum!
          (*And a little amused sniff.*)

Mrs. R.   What message shall I take to him?

Olive.   Tell him not to talk nonsense.

Enter Ayah, *showing in* Colonel Syrett.
            Exit Ayah.

Olive (*to* Syrett, *shaking hands*).   How d'ye do?

Syrett.   How d'ye do?

Olive (*to* Mrs. Remington).   I wish to speak to Colonel Syrett.

Mrs. R.   Don't forget, dear, that the gharry is at the door.   (*To* Syrett.)   Mr. and Mrs. Arnison are just starting for Simla.
                                    (*Exit.*)

Syrett.   I came at once, but I haven't a moment to spare.   How did you know I was here?

OLIVE.   I saw you riding through.   Is there
any news from Fyzapore?

SYRETT.   Yes.   The worst.

OLIVE.   Colonel Carnac has not yet yielded?
He's not dead?

SYRETT.   No.   But there's very little hope.
The Nawab is desperate, half mad.   He knows
that after all his murders there's no chance of
mercy for him, and he has sent a message to
the General to say that unless he and all his
crew are given a free pardon and all their
privileges, he will fire the palace to-morrow
morning and burn and kill everyone in it.

OLIVE.   And where are you going?

SYRETT.   To Fyzapore.

OLIVE.   What for?

SYRETT.   To get inside if I can and tell
Carnac to hold out another day at all costs.
The message came just as the General was
going to fight the Rajah of Sirhoot.   He asked
for a volunteer for Fyzapore.   I offered.

OLIVE.   You offered?

SYRETT.   I have a native servant whom I
can trust, and through him I think I can get
to know what is going on in the Nawab's camp.

OLIVE.   And then what will you do?

SYRETT.   I don't know till I get there.
The General has given me full powers to act
as I think best.

OLIVE. Are you friends with Colonel Carnac?

SYRETT. Yes — at least — on everything except you.

OLIVE. Ah! And about me?

SYRETT. If we both come out of it, I'll try and win you from him.

OLIVE. Colonel Syrett, can I trust you?

SYRETT. In what?

OLIVE. Will you take a letter from me to Colonel Carnac?

SYRETT. You love him? (*She doesn't answer.*) You love him?

OLIVE. Will you take a letter to him?

SYRETT. I shall very likely get taken or killed outside Fyzapore. You wouldn't have your letter found upon me.

(*A little pause,* OLIVE *deliberates.*)

OLIVE. Will you take a message?

SYRETT. Yes.

OLIVE. Faithfully?

SYRETT. Faithfully — if I get to him alive.

OLIVE. Tell Colonel Carnac I have thought of him night and day since he left. I would have come to Fyzapore if I could have got in. Tell him I believe in his luck, and that he will live to come out of this with flying colours. Tell him that I am going to Simla, and that I expect him to join me there the moment he is free. Tell him that if he fails me I will come to him wherever he may be, and I will kill myself at his feet.

SYRETT. As the boy did, with the razor outside your cabin door !

OLIVE. Tell him I will kill myself. Will you give him that message ?

SYRETT. Yes, faithfully. But if I get free I shall come to Simla too ! Do you hear ? I shall come to Simla too !

OLIVE. I can't help your coming to Simla. Take my message to Colonel Carnac.

SYRETT (*goes to her as if to clasp her*). Give me something ! No—let me do this bit of business straight. I'll get through to him if I can. I'll take your message faithfully, and then—promise me that if we both come to Simla you'll give me the same chance to win you that you give to him.

OLIVE. Yes.

SYRETT. Good-bye.   (*Exit*)

Enter MRS. REMINGTON.

MRS. R. Olive, dearest, Charles is in such a fever——

Enter AYAH *with travelling cloak and hat.*

MRS. R. Ah, I'm so glad you are coming—

I'll tell Charles you'll be ready in a minute. (OLIVE *is busy with travelling cloak, and takes no notice.*) You won't be long, dearest, will you?

OLIVE.   I shall be five minutes at least, perhaps ten. (*To* AYAH, *at glass.*) Get me some more gloves, these won't do. (*Dashing them on the floor. Exit* AYAH.) If Charles is in a hurry, tell him please not to wait for me. I will come on to Simla to-morrow — or next week — or next year.

MRS. R. (*very agitated*).   Olive dear, promise me there sha'n't be any scandal?

OLIVE (*at glass*).   Scandal? Scandal? I trust not. I must leave it for him to decide!

> (OLIVE *very deliberately arranges her toilet and then goes off with a very defiant air, followed by* MRS. REMINGTON.)

SCENE III

THE JEWELLED PALACE. NIGHT. PALACE LIGHTED WITH LAMPS AND TORCHES

Discover at table CARNAC, RADNAGE, HOBBS, *and* BARTON, *smoking, with glasses in front of them.*

RADNAGE (*looking at watch, raises glass*). Well, here's hoping that my misspent life may not be brought to an untimely end during the next twenty-four hours, and that we may all quaff and hobnob round this board to-morrow evening.   (*Drinks.*)

BARTON.   And dine together at the Savoy this day twelvemonth !   (*Drinks.*)

HOBBS.   During which time, Dicky, may there be some amendment in your behaviour towards your spiritual supervisors !

(*Drinks.*)

BARTON.   Well, Padri, I promise you I'll never say an unkind word about a parson again (*clapping him affectionately on the shoulder*), and you know (*getting a little sentimental*) I wasn't nearly as good to my mother and sisters as I ought to have been.

RADNAGE.   Ah !   Ah !   Ah !

(*Shaking his head at* BARTON.)

BARTON.   And there was a girl who was fond of me ——

RADNAGE.   Ah !   Ah !   Ah !

(*Shaking his head, solemnly.*)

BARTON.   Well, she was a million times too good for me.   If I do get out of this infernal hole I'll try and be a better man for her sake, eh, sir ?   (*To* CARNAC.)

CARNAC (*who has been a little apart, very anxious and careworn*).   I suppose none of us will be quite the same after this, Dicky, if there is an "after" for us.   I know I shall go out of this place a different man from the man I entered it.

RADNAGE.   Bosh, sir!   Delusive bosh; if I may presume to say so.   Throughout a long and chequered life I have vainly watched for the slightest improvement in my own character, whether induced by the solemn nature of my perpetual good resolutions, or the hell and pickles whereinto my conduct has led me. Padri, my son, it is an amiable fiction of your profession that it can change our characters! Bosh, sir!   Delusive bosh!   Character never changes.   It only develops!   This being so, and no otherwise, we shall go out of this place, if we do go out of it, the very same scamps we entered it, and in six months time we shall probably be very much worse scamps still ——

HOBBS. ⎫
BARTON. ⎬ No, Billy, no!   (*Cries of* "No!")
CARNAC. ⎭

    (*They are all at table listening to* RADNAGE.)

RADNAGE.   I speak for myself.   What is the inference?   Follow me closely, fellow sinners! To whom has my rascally conduct done most damage?   To myself.   Now, upon careful consideration, I have magnanimously forgiven myself.   And if I, who have been so deeply

wronged and injured by my misdoings, can so
freely forgive myself, surely, Padri, your great
Commander-in-Chief won't be outdone in his
own prerogative of mercy by a mere outsider
like me ! Depend upon it, fellow sinners, he'll
think better of the whole business. He'll issue
a free pardon to all of us. Fellow sinners, I
have to stew all night in that poisonous hospital upstairs. I'm going to get a whiff (*sniffs*)
of not very fresh air outside !

> (*Pops off, smoking.* CARNAC *is walking up
> and down in great perplexity.*)

BARTON (*very sympathetically*). I know
you're in a terrible fix, sir.

CARNAC. If I could but hear from the
General. If I could but know whether he
got my last message.

HOBBS. Let me try to cut my way through,
sir. I'll start at once with pleasure.

CARNAC. No, Padri. It may comfort the
women folk to have you near them at the last.

BARTON. Let me go, sir. If I get through,
what shall I say to the General ?

CARNAC. Tell him the state we're in. No
ammunition, the natives in mutiny, the Nawab
desperate. If we're not relieved, any hour may
end it.

BARTON. Yes, sir. Good-bye.

CARNAC. No. Don't go, Dicky.

BARTON. Yes, sir, yes. It's no more dangerous than staying here.

CARNAC. That's true. Very well, my lad, do it. Don't give me the job of breaking the news to your people at home.

(*Exit* BARTON.)

HOBBS. I suppose I shall have to listen in both shafts to-night?

CARNAC. Yes, Padri. If you hear the least sound of any mining, come to me You'll find me here.

Enter ELLICE.

ELLICE. Padri, Mrs. Pennithorne wants to see you.

HOBBS. I was with her for over an hour this morning.

CARNAC. Is she very much worse?

HOBBS. She's always very much worse. The fact is, she's horribly afraid of being blown to bits, and of what will happen to her afterwards. I've done all I can to comfort her.

ELLICE. She thinks she is dying. Go to her, Padri.

HOBBS. Oh, very well. (*Looking at his watch.*) I can give her just ten minutes, and then I must look after my mining shafts.

(*Exit.*)

CARNAC (*to* ELLICE, *who is following him*).
Don't go.   They can do without you for a
few minutes.   (*She stays.*)   I want to speak
to you.

ELLICE.   Yes?

CARNAC.   This has been an awful fortnight
for you.

ELLICE.   No more than for you.   How
changed you are!

CARNAC.   Am I?   What ages it seems
since we came in here!   Yes, I am changed.   I
wanted to tell you ——

ELLICE.   What?

CARNAC.   I daresay it's only the sentimental
cant that we all talk when we are very near
death.   I daresay if we get out of this, I should
be the same worthless fellow I was a month
ago — no, that's not possible — it's not cant — I
don't say it with my tongue — I say it with all
that's sacred in my nature, and I want you to
know before it's too late — if I were to get out
of this, I could never be quite the same man
I have been, I could never run the same danger that you saved me from the other night.
Do you understand?

ELLICE.   Yes.

CARNAC.   Now tell me that you forgive me
for bringing you here.

ELLICE   Forgive you?   I thank you.

CARNAC. For bringing you to die?

ELLICE. With them — with you. And you don't think the end will be very horrible?

CARNAC. I trust not.

ELLICE. How do you think it will come?

CARNAC. We may be all butchered or shot at any moment. The Nawab is mad with fury — one can scarcely tell what may happen — suppose I see that you may meet with some horrible cruelty before death, you would trust yourself to me ——

ELLICE. Yes. Kill me yourself.

CARNAC. This is the saddest night you have ever spent ——

ELLICE. No, I am very happy.

FORD *enters quickly.*

FORD. Poor Radnage! He wants to see you, sir.

CARNAC. What is it?

FORD. Mr. Barton crept out to get through the enemy's lines and was fired at. Billy Radnage saw him fall, ran out, and dragged him in, got him just to the gate when he was shot himself.

CARNAC. Both killed?

FORD. No, Barton's wound is very slight. But Billy says it's all over with himself.

Enter RADNAGE, *supported by two* SOLDIERS.

RADNAGE.   That's so.   (*To the* SOLDIERS.)
Pin me up, you boys.   (*To* CARNAC.)   Colonel ——

CARNAC.   Billy, I'd rather it had been
myself !

RADNAGE.   Nonsense.   Thank God, I'm
spared a cruel old age. Colonel, Miss Ford ——
(*To the* SOLDIERS.)   Give me a spoonful of
something, you boys — when I dropped just
now I kept on hearing old psalm-singer's dying
words.   You remember that night at the Club
when he joined your hands.   (CARNAC *and*
ELLICE *look at each other.*)   If I'm wrong, laugh
at me for a silly fool and bury it with all my
other follies — but — I'm going to try and
wriggle into old psalm-singer's family Paradise
— I know it's a forlorn hope, but if St. Peter
isn't looking I may squeeze in on the sly, and
if I do, shall I take old psalm-singer any
message, Colonel ?

CARNAC (*holds out his hand to* ELLICE, *who re-
sponds, at the same time saying to* FORD).   Mr.
Ford, if this were a time, wouldyou give her
to me ?

(FORD *nods, and in dumb motion gives her
to* CARNAC, *who takes her hand.*)

CARNAC.   If we live, Billy — if we live ——

RADNAGE.   Drink one glass with me, old
friend, before I start. (*They give him a glass.*
CARNAC *also takes one.*) Wish me a prosperous
voyage, and here's to you — with as long life
as God may see fit. (*Drinks.*) Sorry I can't
do any more for those poor devils in hospital.
My love to all the boys and all the girls — ah !
the plaguey creatures ! And the merry drink !
I've had a good time ! It's only a few minutes,
boys. Take me to the shed (*they take him up*)
and lay me beside the other past masters. (*As
he is taken off he calls out.*) Tell General
Scrivener I've sent in my papers l I've made a
good end, haven't I !

> (*They are taking him off,* CARNAC *following,*
> *when* LOVATT *enters in great excitement.*
> RADNAGE *is taken off, all of them following.*)

LOVATT.   Sir, Colonel Syrett has got through
the enemy's lines. He has just come in.

CARNAC.   Syrett !

Enter SYRETT *in native dress.*

CARNAC.   Syrett ! How did you get in ?
                              (*Exit* LOVATT.)

SYRETT.   Crept through in this dress, with
the help of my servant.

CARNAC.   What news ? Has the General
fought the Rajah of Sirhoot ?

SYRETT.   I left him just as he was going into
the fight.   He asked for a volunteer to come
here.   I offered because I wanted to wipe out
what I did the other night ——

CARNAC.   Hush! That's forgotten! (*Offers
hand.   A warm handshake between the two men.*)
When can he send to relieve us?

SYRETT.   If he is victorious he'll make a
forced march here as soon as the fight is over.
But it's hopeless!

CARNAC.   Why!

SYRETT.   I had a servant with me whom I
could trust.   I sent him into the Nawab's tent
to learn what he could.

CARNAC.   Well?

SYRETT.   The Nawab means to make one
last try to get you to give yourselves up as
hostages.   He's mad and drunk, and if you
do surrender it's likely we shall all be treach-
erously murdered.   If you don't surrender he
means to bombard the Palace to-morrow morning.   Can you defend it?

CARNAC.   No.   All the powder's gone.

SYRETT.   Then it's all up with us.

CARNAC.   Looks like it.

SYRETT.   I have a message for you.

CARNAC.   From whom?

SYRETT.   Mrs. Arnison.

CARNAC.   Mrs. Arnison? I'd rather not hear

it. It's years since I saw her. I have forgotten her.

SYRETT. Is that so? Let me give my
message faithfully, as I promised. She says
she has thought of you day and night since
you left. She says she believes in your luck,
and that you'll come out of this with flying
colours. She says she is going to Simla, and
that if you don't come to her——

ELLICE *has entered and come up to them.*

ELLICE. Poor Billy has gone! He sends
his love to you, and hopes you won't meet
Mr. Funk when it comes to the end. Colonel
Syrett!

SYRETT. Miss Ford!

ELLICE. Are we to be relieved?

SYRETT. The General will do his best——

Enter CAPTAIN BELL.

BELL. A messenger from the Nawab, sir.

CARNAC. Show him in, Captain Bell.

    (CARNAC *sits to receive the* MESSENGER.)

Enter LOVATT *with* NAWAB'S MESSENGER. MES-
    SENGER *salaams,* CARNAC *bows.*

MESSENGER. Carnac Sahib, the glorious and

mighty Nawab of Fyzapore, sends his salaam.
He asks you for the last time to place yourself and all the soldiers and the Memsahibs
under his protection as hostages to the English Government.

CARNAC.   Tell his Highness that I await
General Scrivener's commands.   Till I receive
them I hold this Palace for Her Majesty.

MESSENGER.   Under what condition will you
surrender the Palace to his Highness?

CARNAC.   Under no conditions whatever.

MESSENGER (*salaams*).   Then his Highness
will attack the Palace to-morrow morning,
and he will spare not a single life.

CARNAC.   Captain Bell, conduct his Highness's messenger to the gate, and see that he
is not fired upon. (*Exit* BELL *and* MESSEN-
GER.)   Mr. Lovatt, go round to everyone in
the Palace and say that we may expect to be
attacked at sunrise.   Say that I rely that
there will be no alarm or confusion, but that
everybody will be found in readiness at his
post.

LOVATT.   Yes, sir.   (*Exit.*)

ELLICE.   You think it is the end?

CARNAC.   I fear it.   Try and get some rest.

ELLICE.   I couldn't sleep.   Promise me one
last thing.

CARNAC.   It's done.   What is it?

ELLICE. You are worn to death. We all depend on you. Get some sleep. I'll watch for you and call you the moment you are wanted. (*He demurs.*)   Yes — please — you have promised.

CARNAC. I think I could go off. (*Comes up to table.*)   Arthur — will you watch with her for an hour?

SYRETT. Yes, sir.

CARNAC (*holding hand*).   Good fellow! You've only come in to die with us ——

SYRETT (*warm handshake*).   I thought it might come to that.

> (CARNAC *sighs deeply with fatigue, and drops on a couch.*)

CARNAC. I am dead beat ——

> (*Falls asleep.*)

> (ELLICE *watches* CARNAC, *fanning him. The curtain falls. The curtain remains down for a few seconds to signify the passing of the night.*)

SCENE IV

SCENE THE SAME. DAWN, SCARCELY LIGHT. IT
GROWS LIGHTER DURING THE SCENE.

Discover CARNAC *asleep.* SYRETT *enters, looking off.
Great shouting and noise.*

SYRETT (*to* ELLICE). Yes! Wake him up!
It's quite true.

ELLICE. Colonel Carnac! Wake! Wake!
Do you hear! Will you wake!

CARNAC (*stirs*). What is it? Where am I?

ELLICE. Such good news! We're all saved!
Do you hear? We are saved! The General
has won a great victory, and the Nawab's
troops have mutinied against him and killed
him! We're saved! It's true!

CARNAC. Am I dead, or dreaming, or —
what is it?

ELLICE. We're saved! The Nawab's killed!
The General has done a forced march all
through the night! Look! He's here!

Enter GENERAL SCRIVENER, *his staff*, SYRETT,
BARTON, LOVATT, BELL, MADGE LOVELACE,
MAY FORD, HOBBS, *etc.*

SCRIVENER. All well here, Colonel Carnac?

CARNAC (*salutes*). All well, sir.

CURTAIN.

www.ingramcontent.com/pod-product-compliance
Lightning Source LLC
Chambersburg PA
CBHW021129020726
47500CB00003B/994